DATE DUE

DEC

PRAISE FOR squish!

"Even the mildest young boy will see something of himself in Squish. *Super Amoeba* is an energetic, good-hearted escapade, one that young readers will enjoy."
—*The New York Times*

★"The hilarious misadventures of a hapless young everylad who happens to be an amoeba. If ever a new series deserved to go viral, this one does."
—*Kirkus Reviews*, Starred

"The Holms strike a breezy, goofy tone right out of the gate."
—*Publishers Weekly*

"A perfect mix of writing that is simple enough for early readers but still remarkably snarky, clever, and entertaining. . . . Kids themselves will soak up the humor, tidbits of science instruction, and adventure."
—*The Bulletin of the Center for Children's Books*

"A new graphic novel series that will have readers everywhere clapping their pseudopods in glee. There's some real science worked in here too and even directions for a kid-friendly experiment."
—*Bookends* (*Booklist* blog)

Read ALL the SQUISH books!

#1 SQUISH: Super Amoeba

#2 SQUISH: Brave New Pond

#3 SQUISH: The Power of the Parasite

#4 SQUISH: Captain Disaster

squish
CAPTAIN DISASTER

BY JENNIFER L. HOLM & MATTHEW HOLM

RANDOM HOUSE 🏠 NEW YORK

All rights reserved. Published in the United States by Random House Children's Books, a division of Random House, Inc., New York.

Random House and the colophon are registered trademarks of Random House, Inc.

Visit us on the Web! randomhouse.com/kids

Educators and librarians, for a variety of teaching tools, visit us at RHTeachersLibrarians.com

Library of Congress Cataloging-in-Publication Data
Holm, Jennifer L.
Captain Disaster / by Jennifer L. Holm & Matthew Holm. —
1st ed.   p. cm. — (Squish ; #4)
Summary: Squish, comic book fan and grade school amoeba, is made captain of his soccer team and following the example of his favorite superhero, must figure out how to turn a losing streak around without losing his friends.
ISBN 978-0-375-84392-1 (trade pbk.) —
ISBN 978-0-375-93786-6 (lib. bdg.)
1. Graphic novels. [1. Graphic novels. 2. Amoeba—Fiction.
3. Soccer—Fiction. 4. Teamwork (Sports)—Fiction.
5. Superheroes—Fiction.] I. Holm, Matthew. II. Title.
PZ7.7.H65Cap 2012   741.5'973—dc23   2011041155

MANUFACTURED IN MALAYSIA   10 9 8 7 6 5 4 3 2 1
First Edition

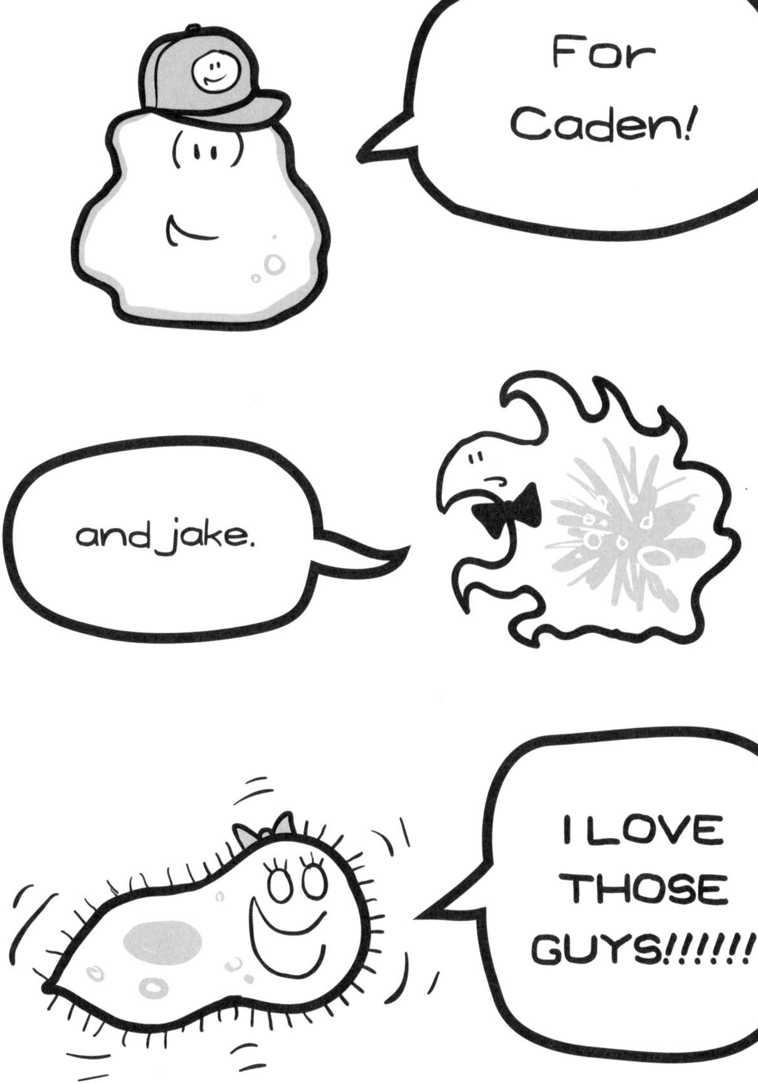
For Caden!
and jake.
I LOVE THOSE GUYS!!!!!!

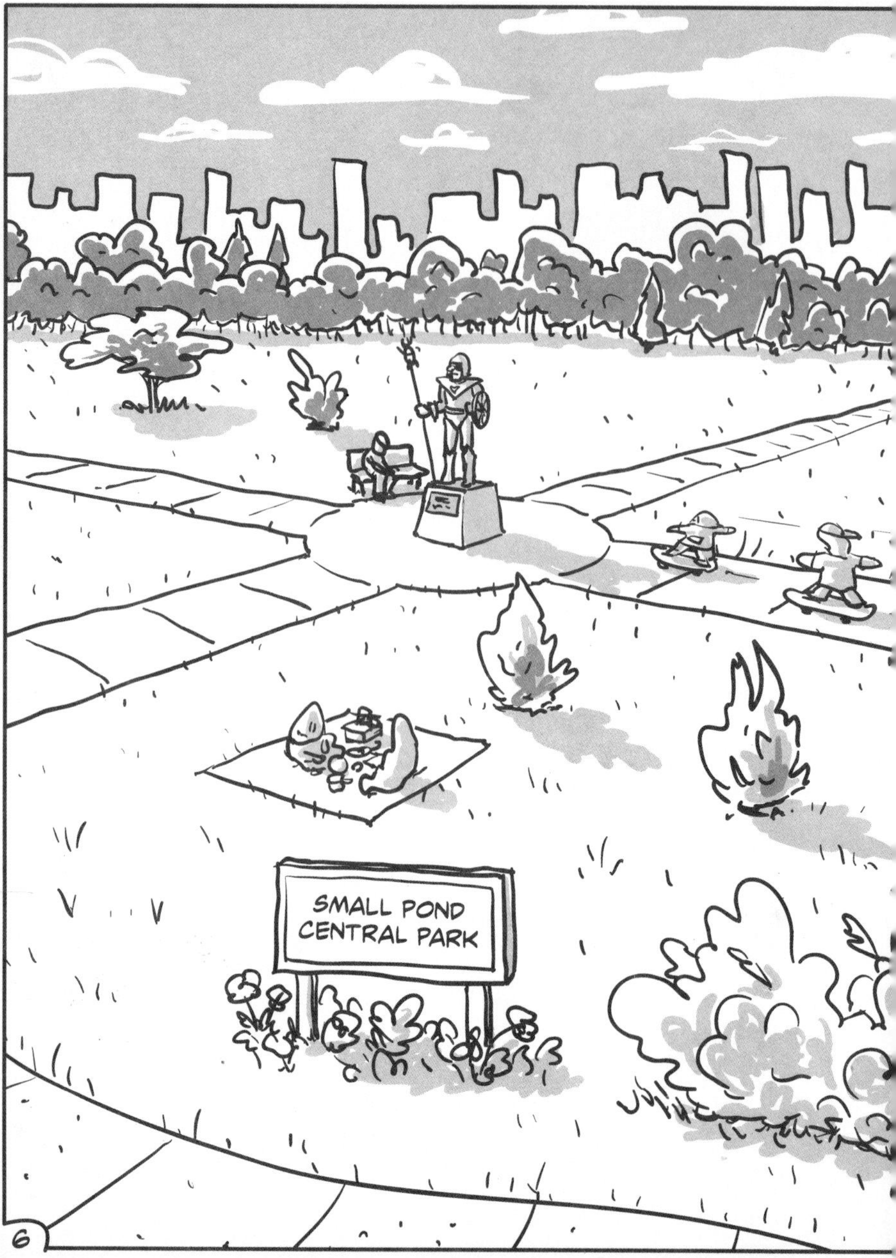
SMALL POND
CENTRAL PARK

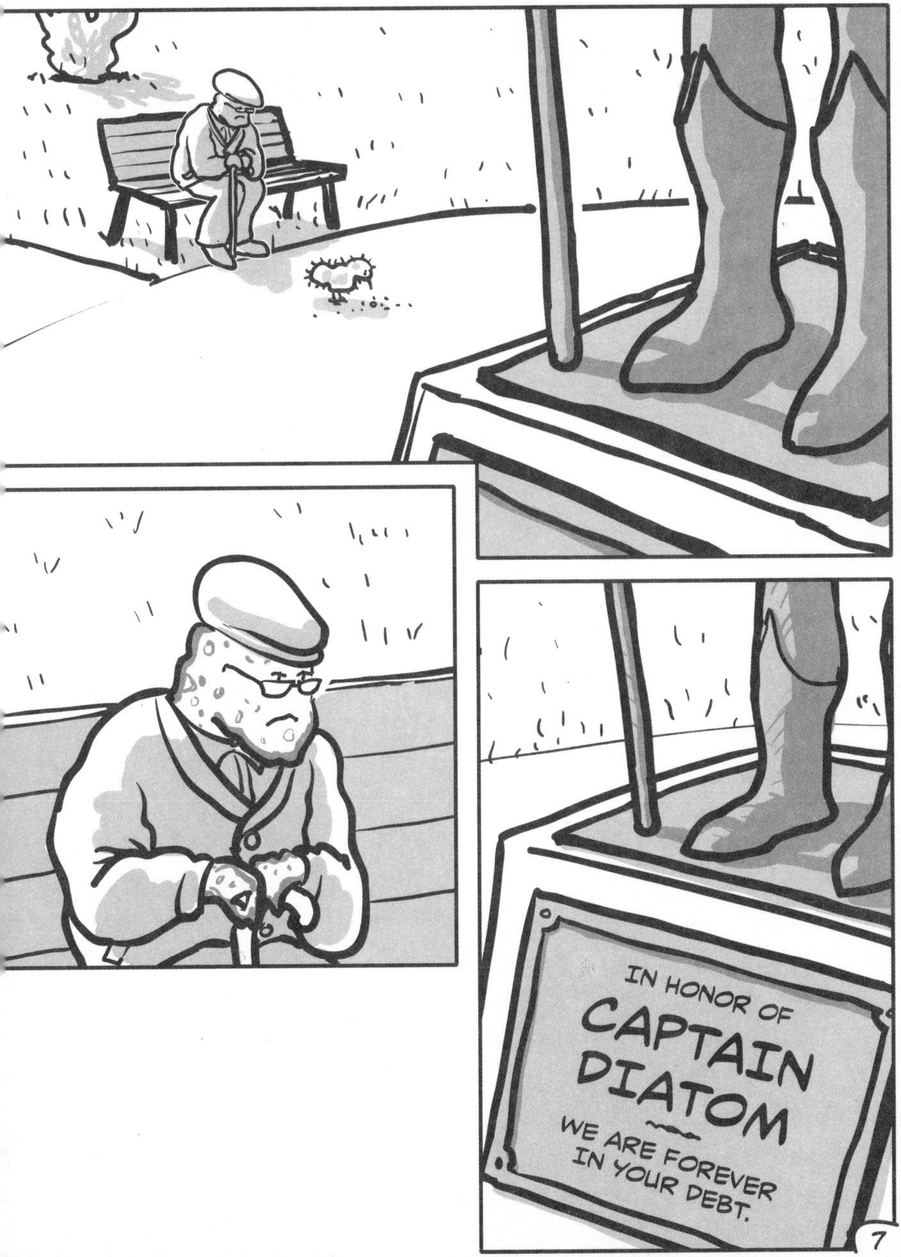

IN HONOR OF
CAPTAIN DIATOM
WE ARE FOREVER IN YOUR DEBT.

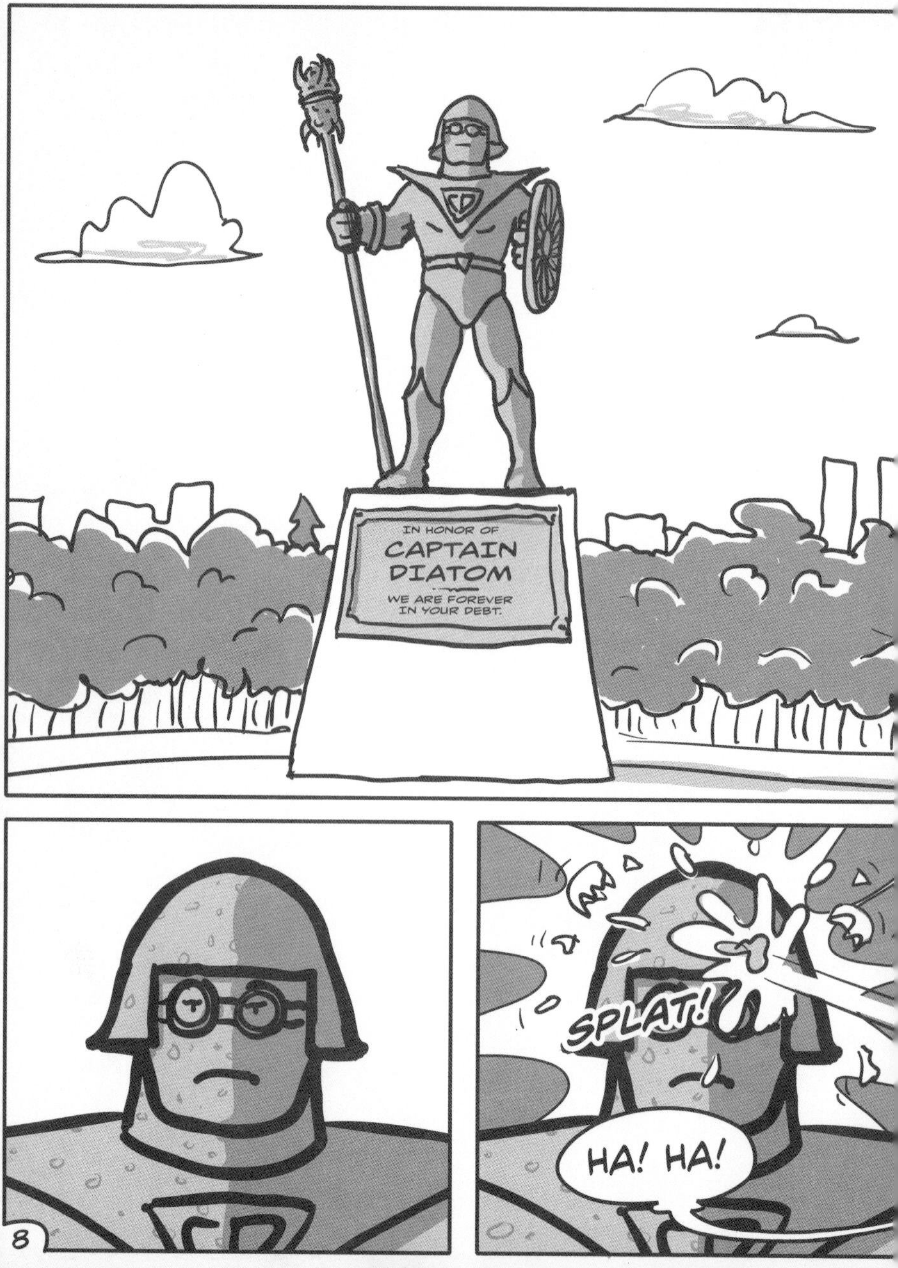
IN HONOR OF
CAPTAIN DIATOM
WE ARE FOREVER IN YOUR DEBT.
SPLAT!
HA! HA!

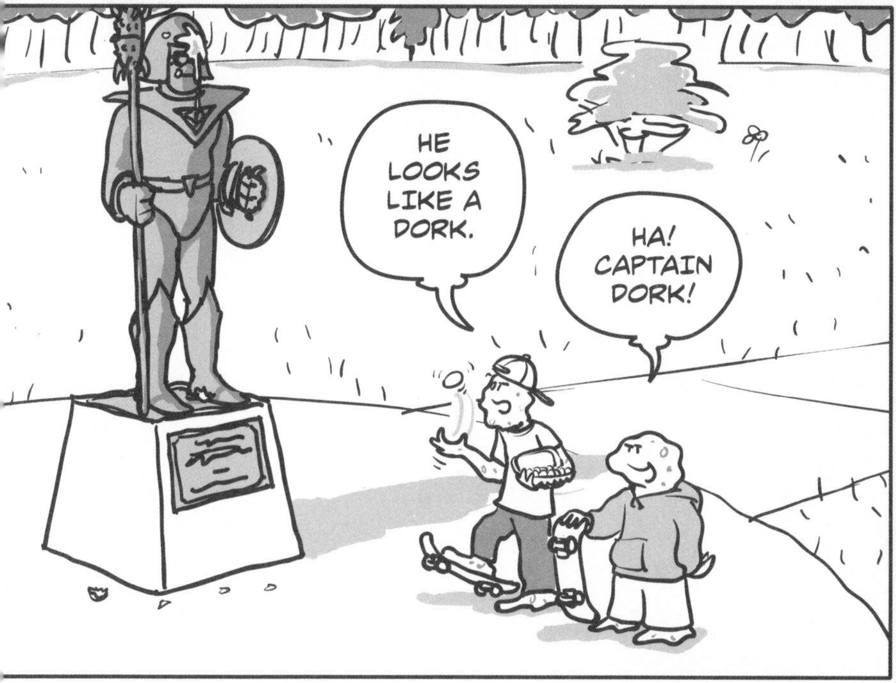
HE LOOKS LIKE A DORK.
HA! CAPTAIN DORK!

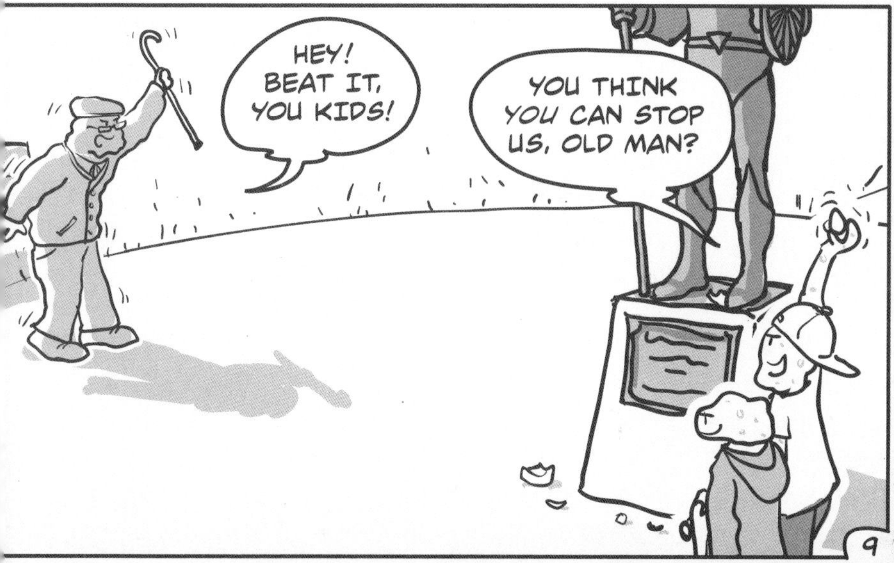
HEY! BEAT IT, YOU KIDS!
YOU THINK YOU CAN STOP US, OLD MAN?

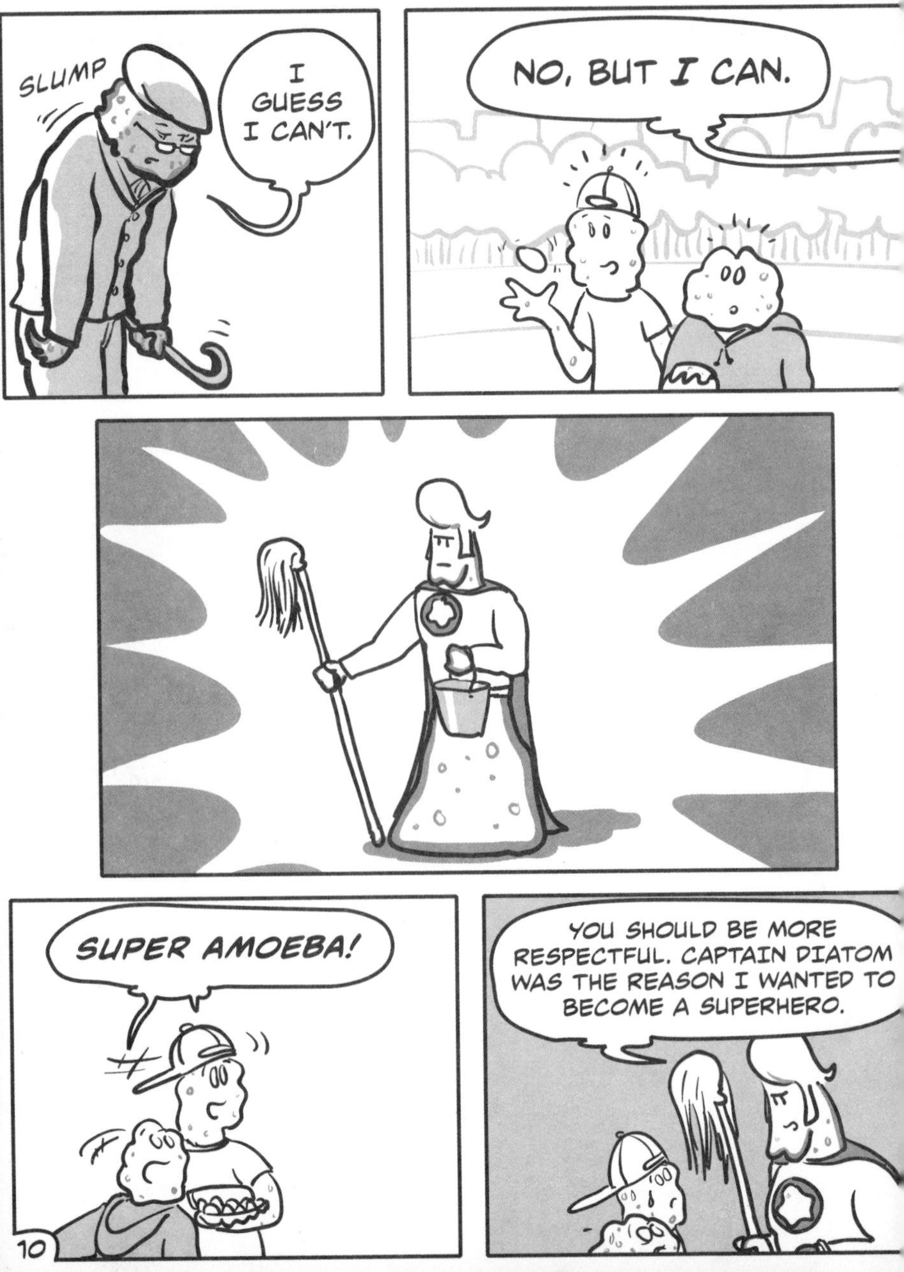
SLUMP
I GUESS I CAN'T.
NO, BUT *I* CAN.
SUPER AMOEBA!
YOU SHOULD BE MORE RESPECTFUL. CAPTAIN DIATOM WAS THE REASON I WANTED TO BECOME A SUPERHERO.

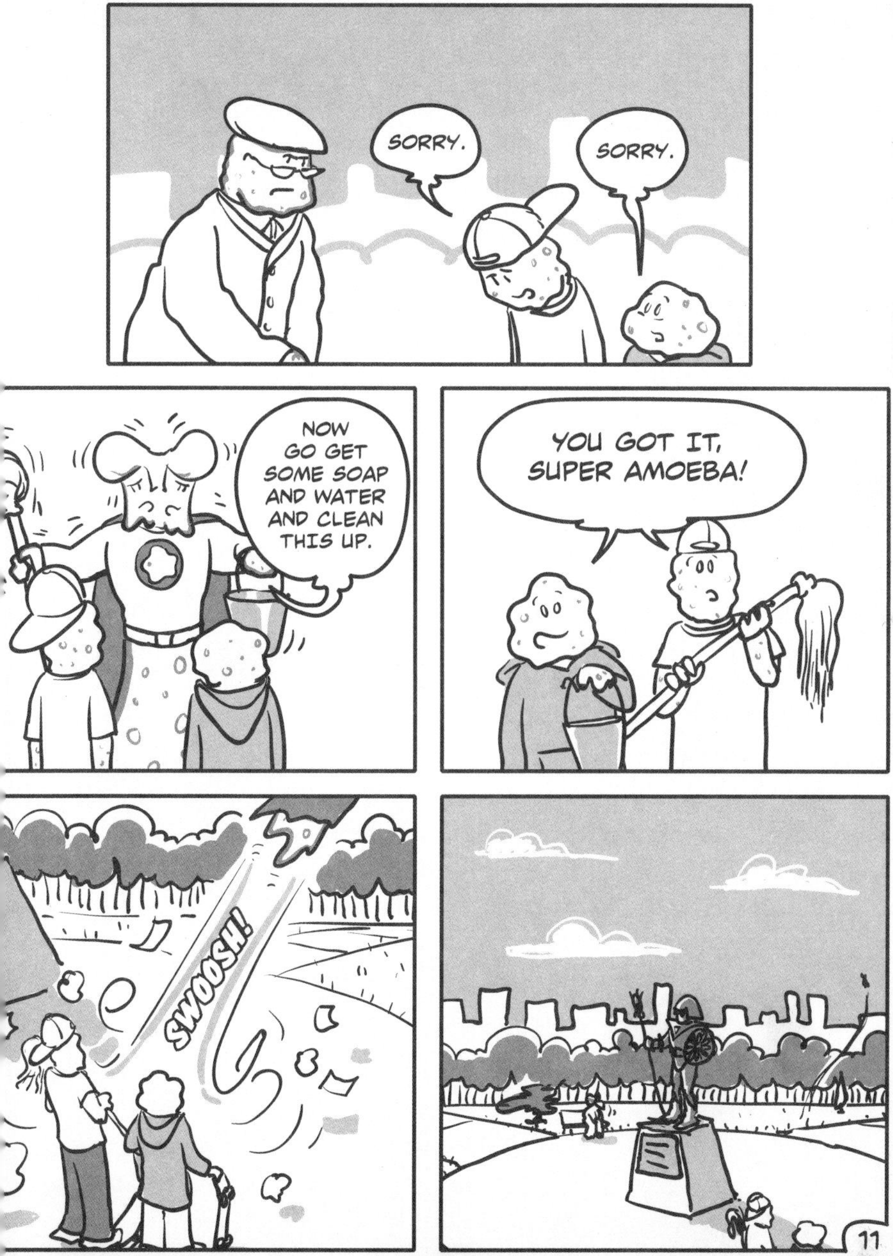
SORRY.
SORRY.
NOW GO GET SOME SOAP AND WATER AND CLEAN THIS UP.
YOU GOT IT, SUPER AMOEBA!
SWOOSH!

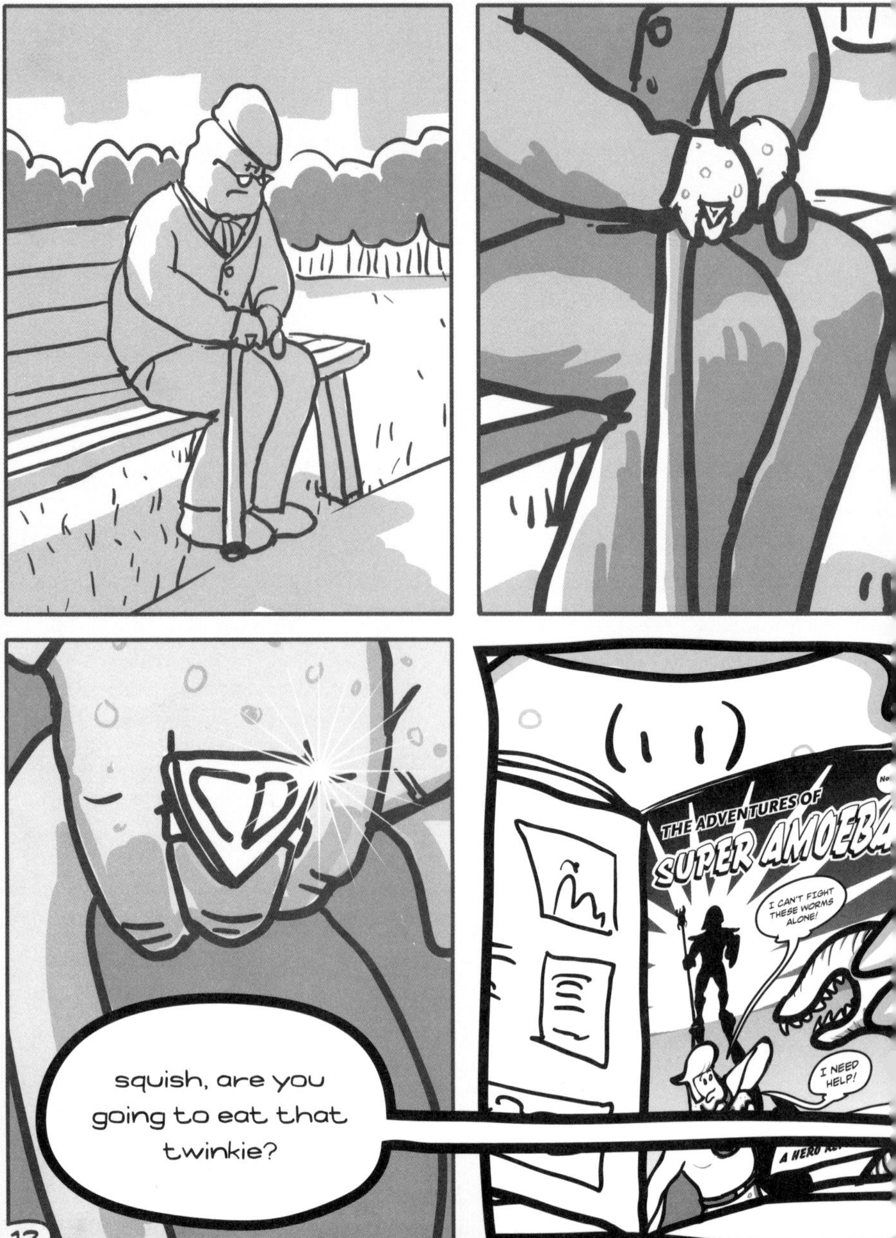
squish, are you going to eat that twinkie?
THE ADVENTURES OF
SUPER AMOEB
I CAN'T FIGHT THESE WORMS ALONE!
I NEED HELP!

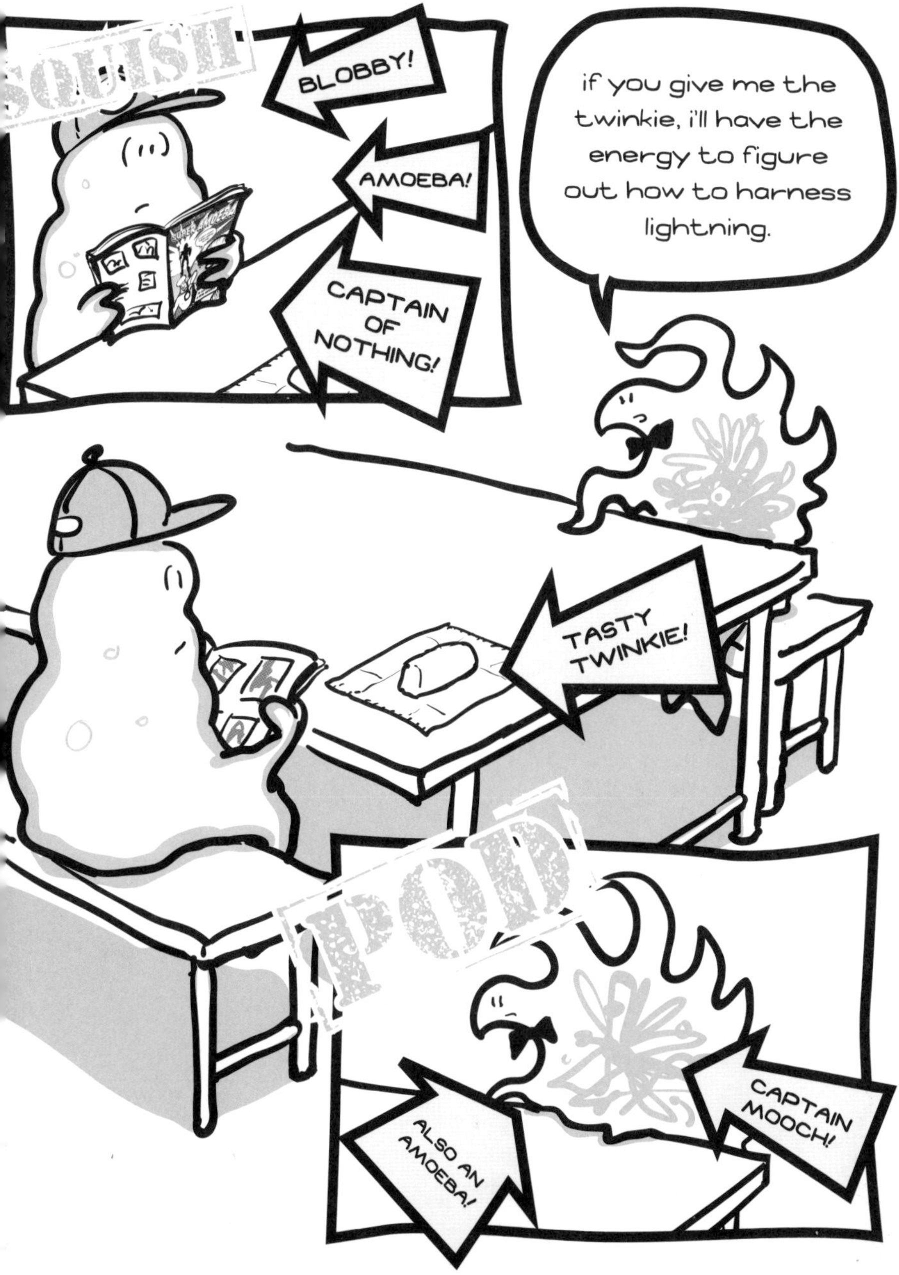
SQUISH
BLOBBY!
AMOEBA!
CAPTAIN OF NOTHING!
if you give me the twinkie, i'll have the energy to figure out how to harness lightning.
TASTY TWINKIE!
POP
ALSO AN AMOEBA!
CAPTAIN MOOCH!

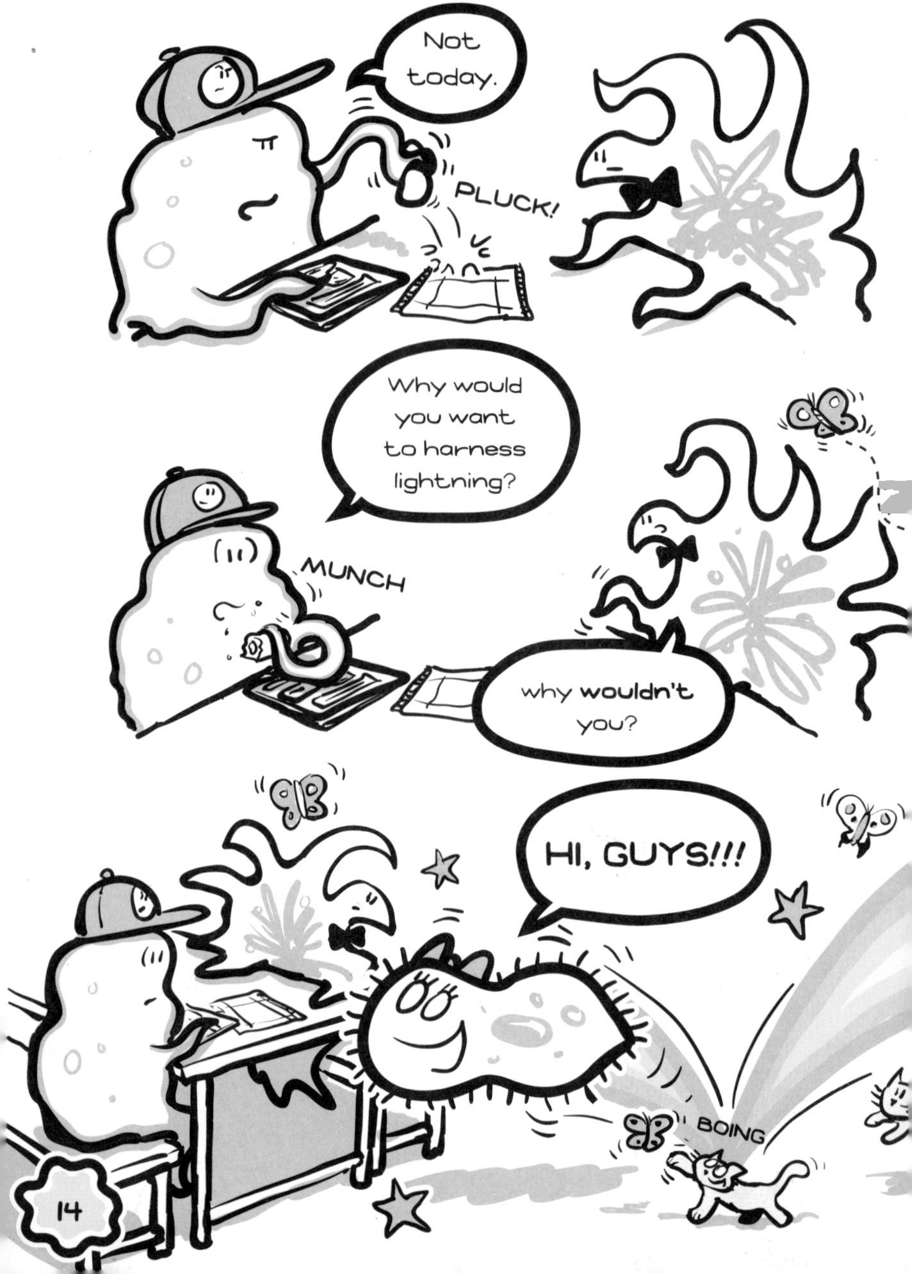
Not today.
PLUCK!
Why would you want to harness lightning?
MUNCH
why wouldn't you?
HI, GUYS!!!
BOING

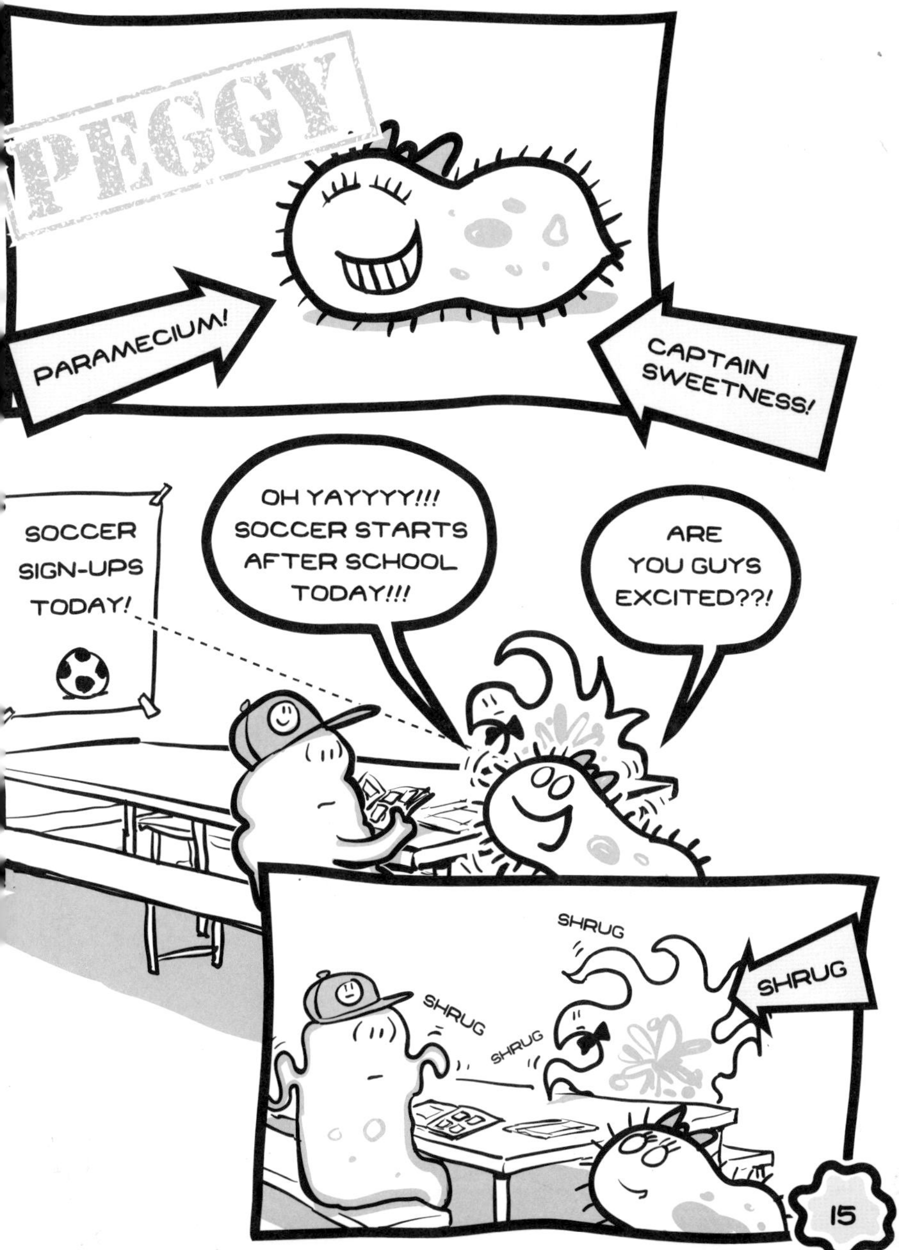
PEGGY
PARAMECIUM!
CAPTAIN SWEETNESS!
SOCCER SIGN-UPS TODAY!
OH YAYYYY!!! SOCCER STARTS AFTER SCHOOL TODAY!!!
ARE YOU GUYS EXCITED??!
SHRUG
SHRUG
SHRUG
SHRUG

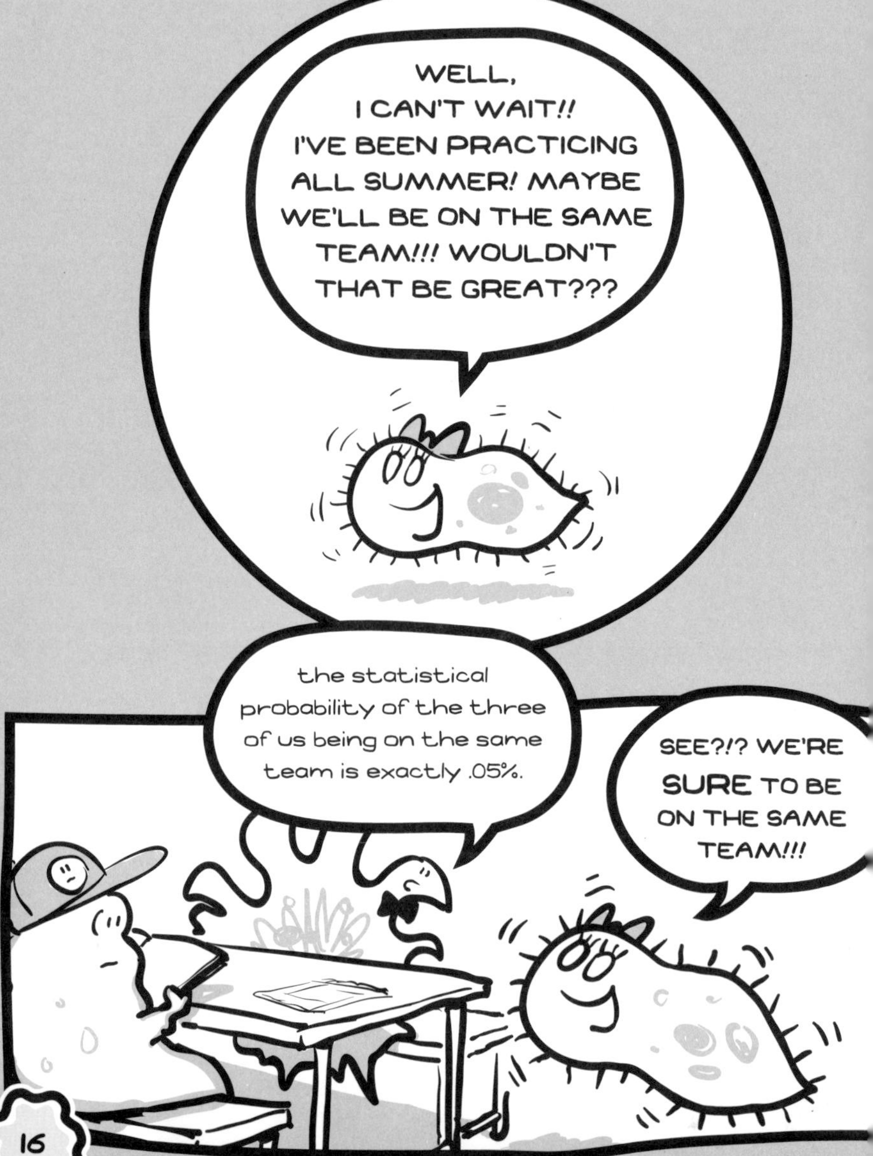

WELL, I CAN'T WAIT!! I'VE BEEN PRACTICING ALL SUMMER! MAYBE WE'LL BE ON THE SAME TEAM!!! WOULDN'T THAT BE GREAT???
the statistical probability of the three of us being on the same team is exactly .05%.
SEE?!? WE'RE SURE TO BE ON THE SAME TEAM!!!

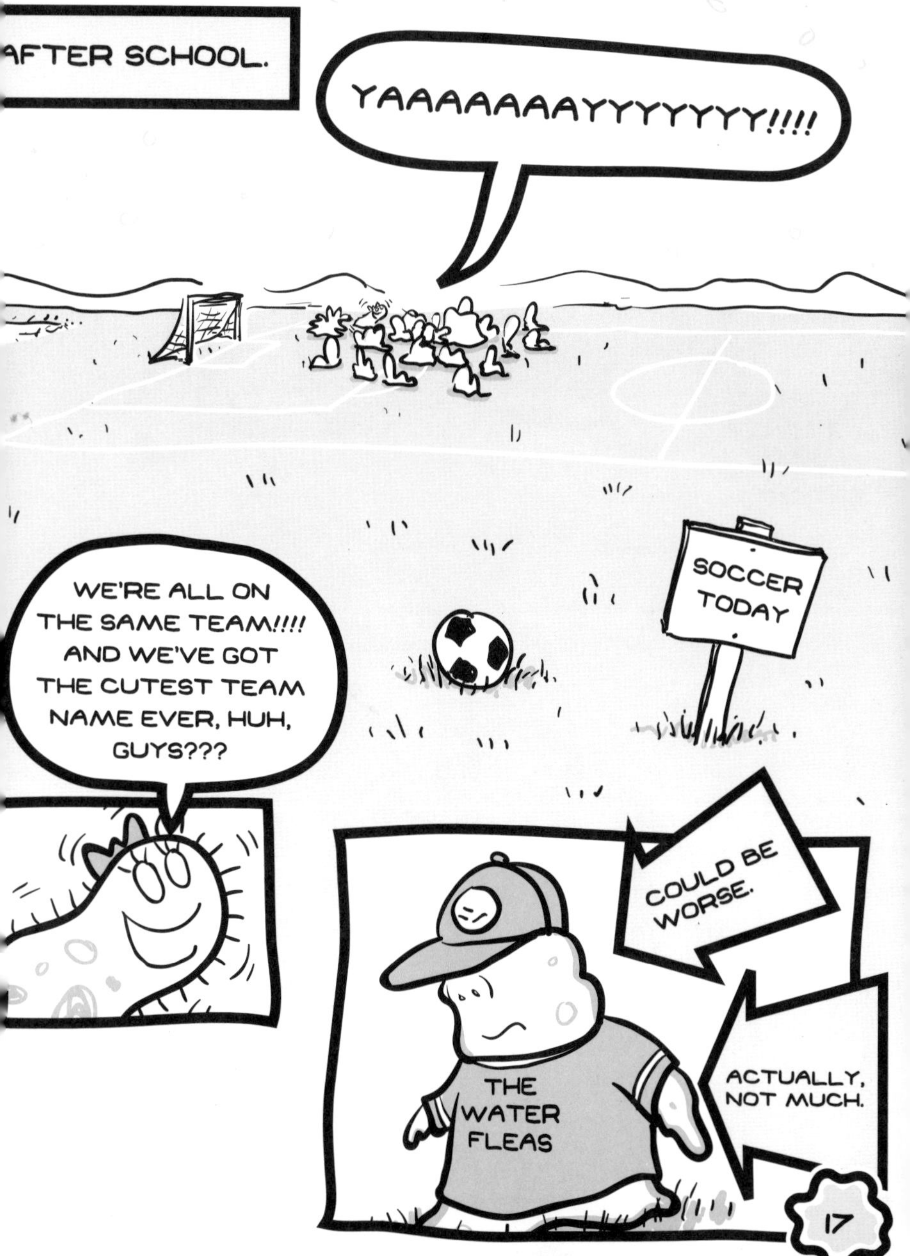
AFTER SCHOOL.
YAAAAAAAAYYYYYYYY!!!!
SOCCER TODAY
WE'RE ALL ON THE SAME TEAM!!!! AND WE'VE GOT THE CUTEST TEAM NAME EVER, HUH, GUYS???
COULD BE WORSE.
THE WATER FLEAS
ACTUALLY, NOT MUCH.

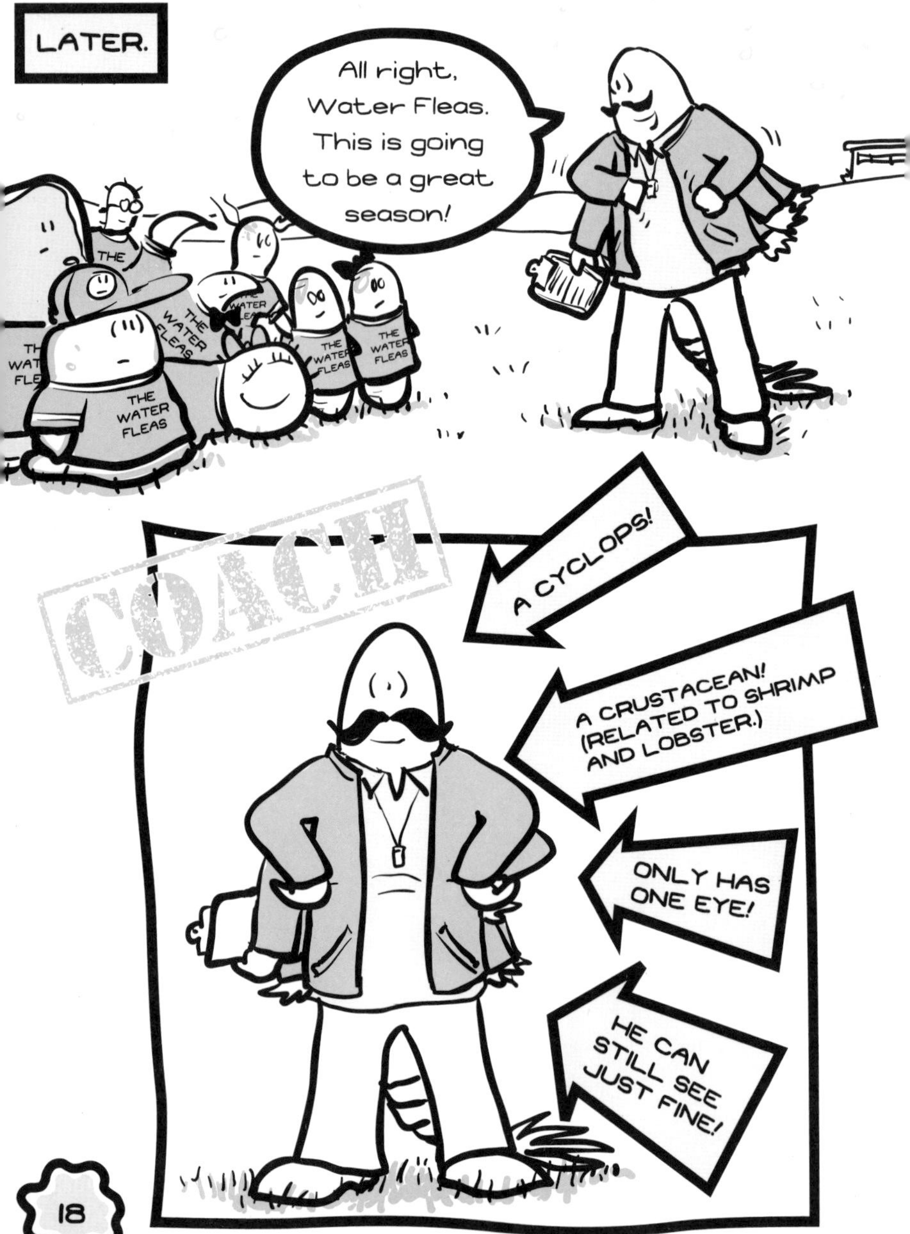
LATER.
All right, Water Fleas. This is going to be a great season!
THE WATER FLEAS
COACH
A CYCLOPS!
A CRUSTACEAN! (RELATED TO SHRIMP AND LOBSTER.)
ONLY HAS ONE EYE!
HE CAN STILL SEE JUST FINE!

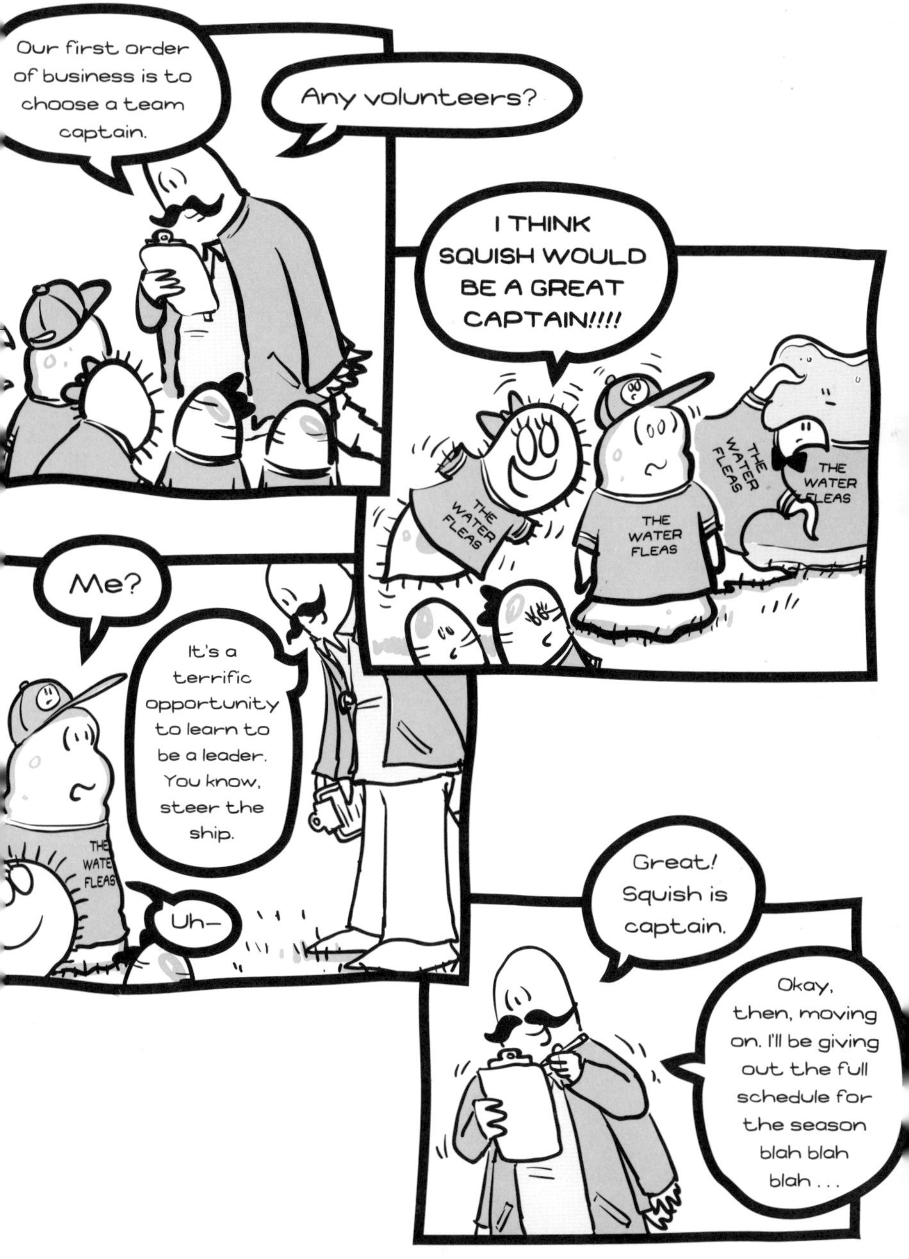
Our first order of business is to choose a team captain.
Any volunteers?
I THINK SQUISH WOULD BE A GREAT CAPTAIN!!!!
THE WATER FLEAS
THE WATER FLEAS
THE WATER FLEAS
THE WATER FLEAS
Me?
It's a terrific opportunity to learn to be a leader. You know, steer the ship.
THE WATER FLEAS
Uh—
Great! Squish is captain.
Okay, then, moving on. I'll be giving out the full schedule for the season blah blah blah . . .

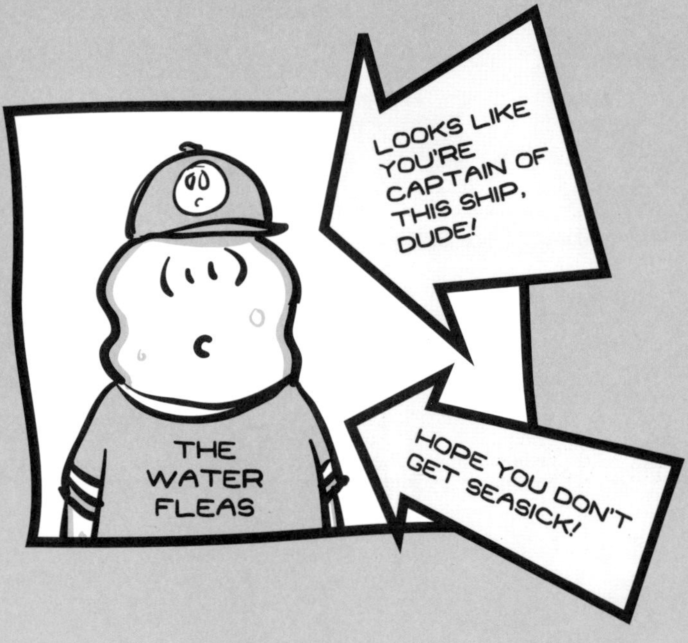
THE WATER FLEAS
LOOKS LIKE YOU'RE CAPTAIN OF THIS SHIP, DUDE!
HOPE YOU DON'T GET SEASICK!

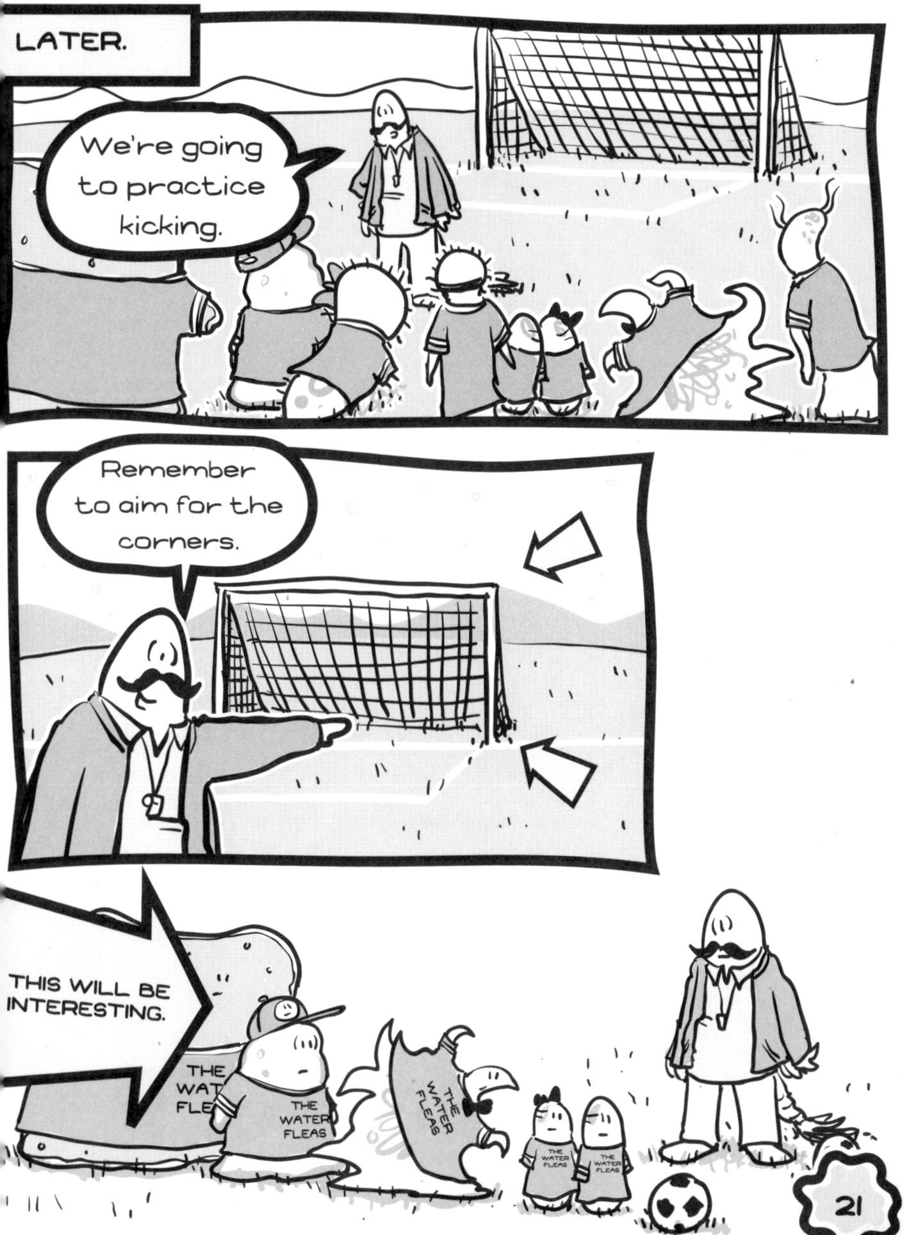
LATER.
We're going to practice kicking.
Remember to aim for the corners.
THIS WILL BE INTERESTING.
THE WAT FLE
THE WATER FLEAS
THE WATER FLEAS
THE WATER FLEAS
THE WATER FLEAS

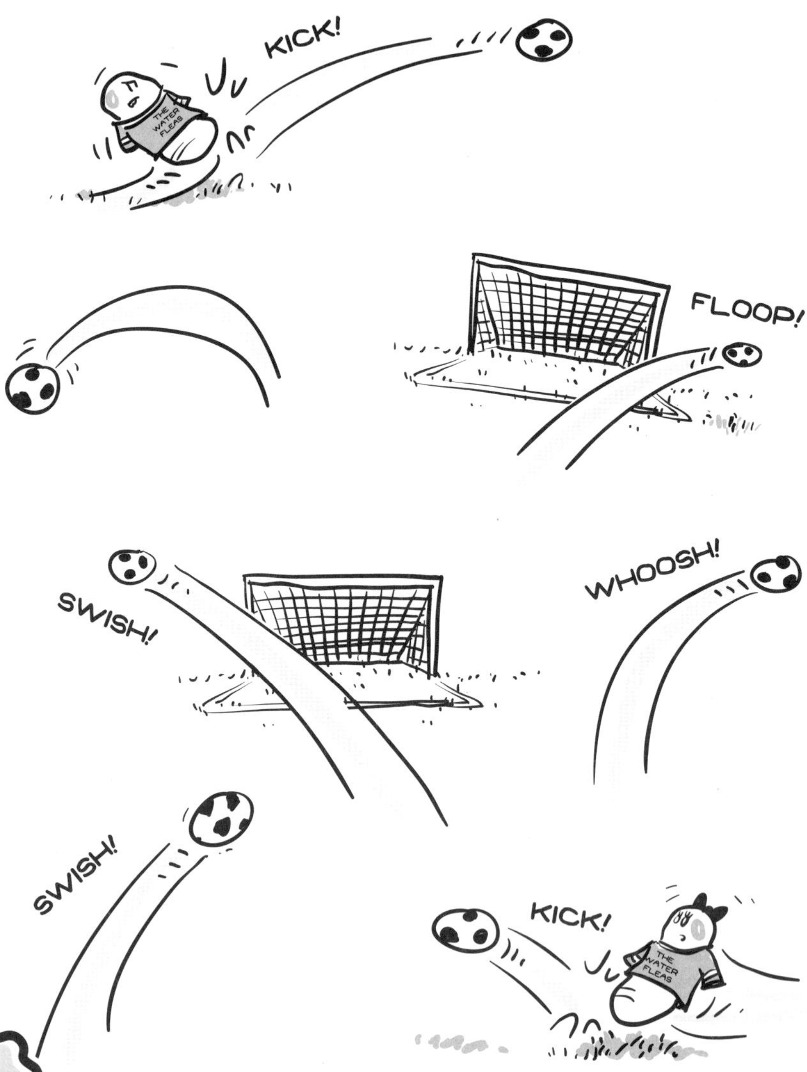
KICK!
THE WATER FLEAS
FLOOP!
SWISH!
WHOOSH!
SWISH!
KICK!
THE WATER FLEAS

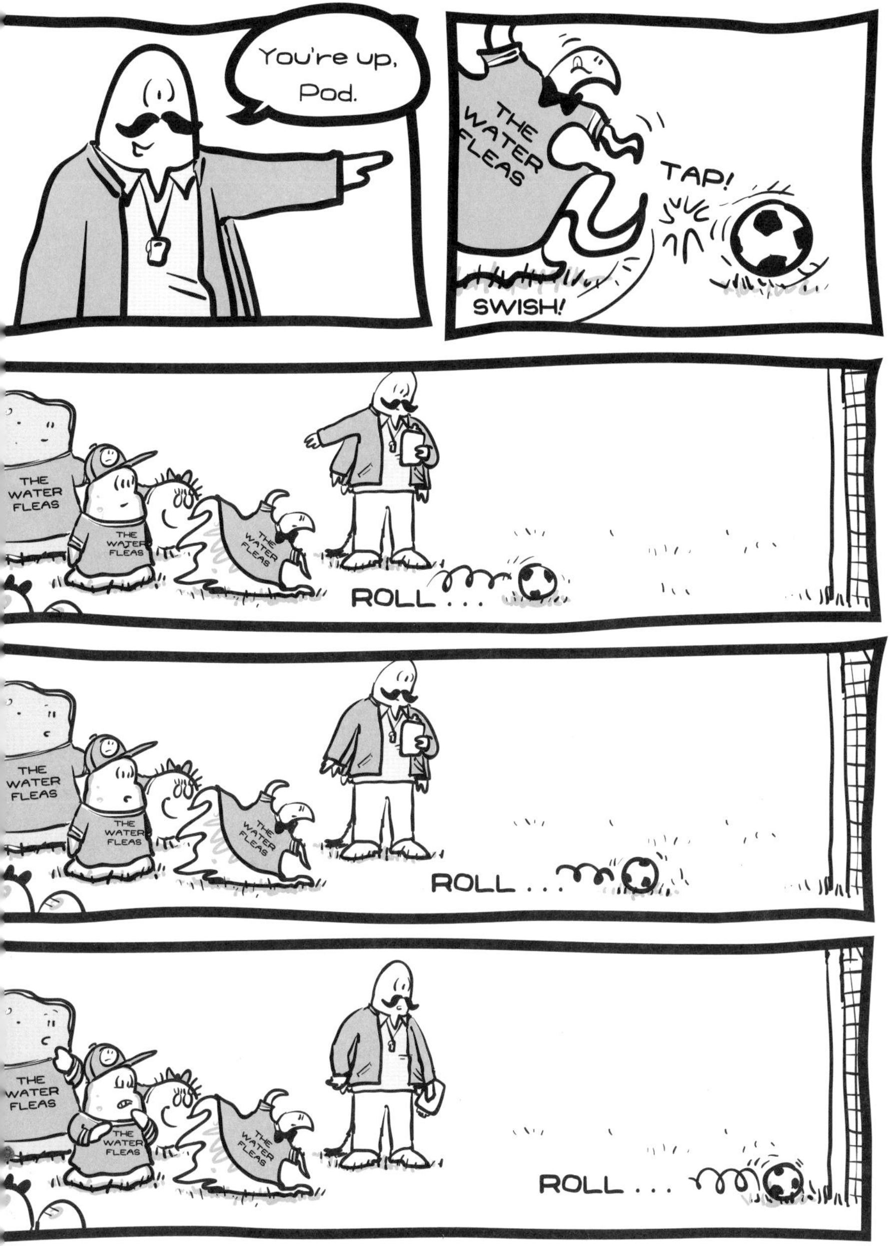
You're up, Pod.
THE WATER FLEAS
TAP!
SWISH!
THE WATER FLEAS
THE WATER FLEAS
THE WATER FLEAS
ROLL . . .
THE WATER FLEAS
THE WATER FLEAS
THE WATER FLEAS
ROLL . . .
THE WATER FLEAS
THE WATER FLEAS
THE WATER FLEAS
ROLL . . .

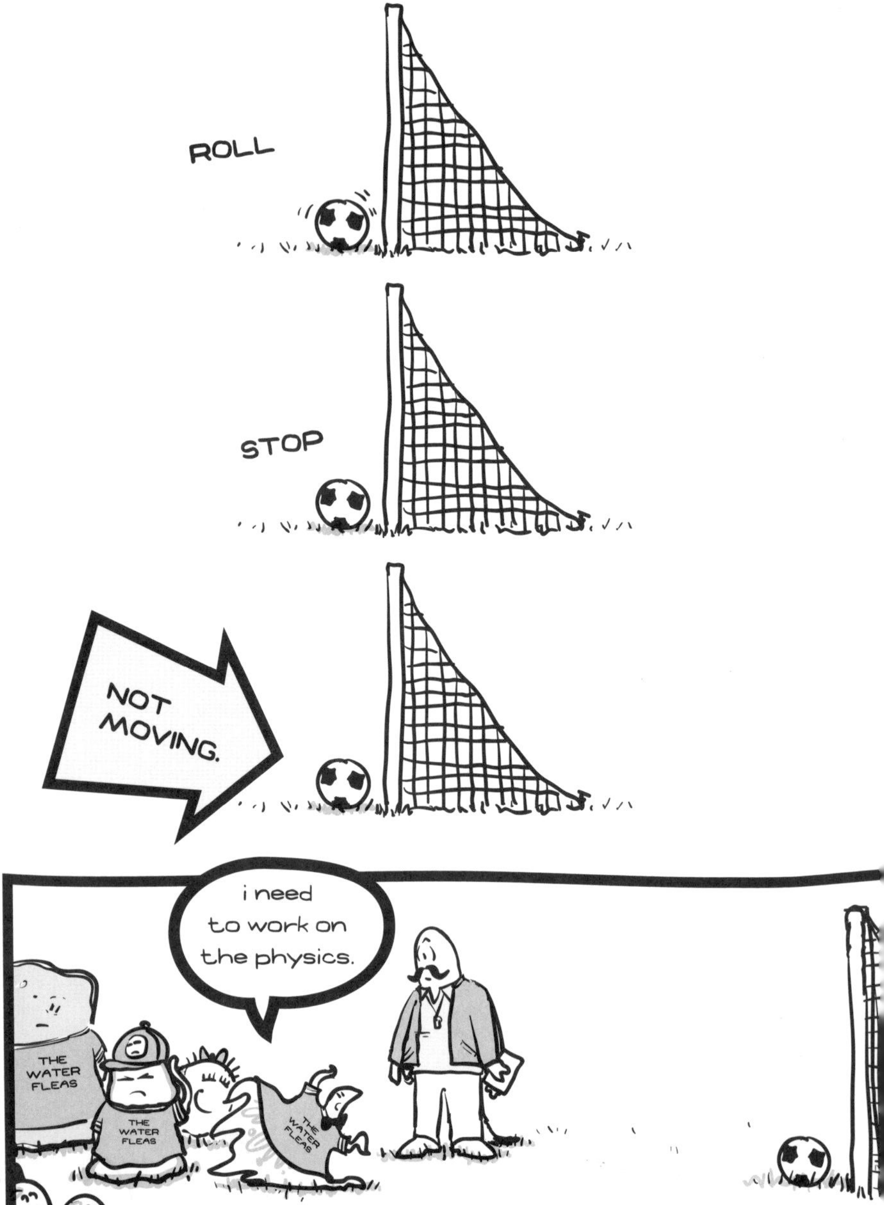
ROLL
STOP
NOT MOVING.
i need to work on the physics.
THE WATER FLEAS
THE WATER FLEAS
THE WATER FLEAS

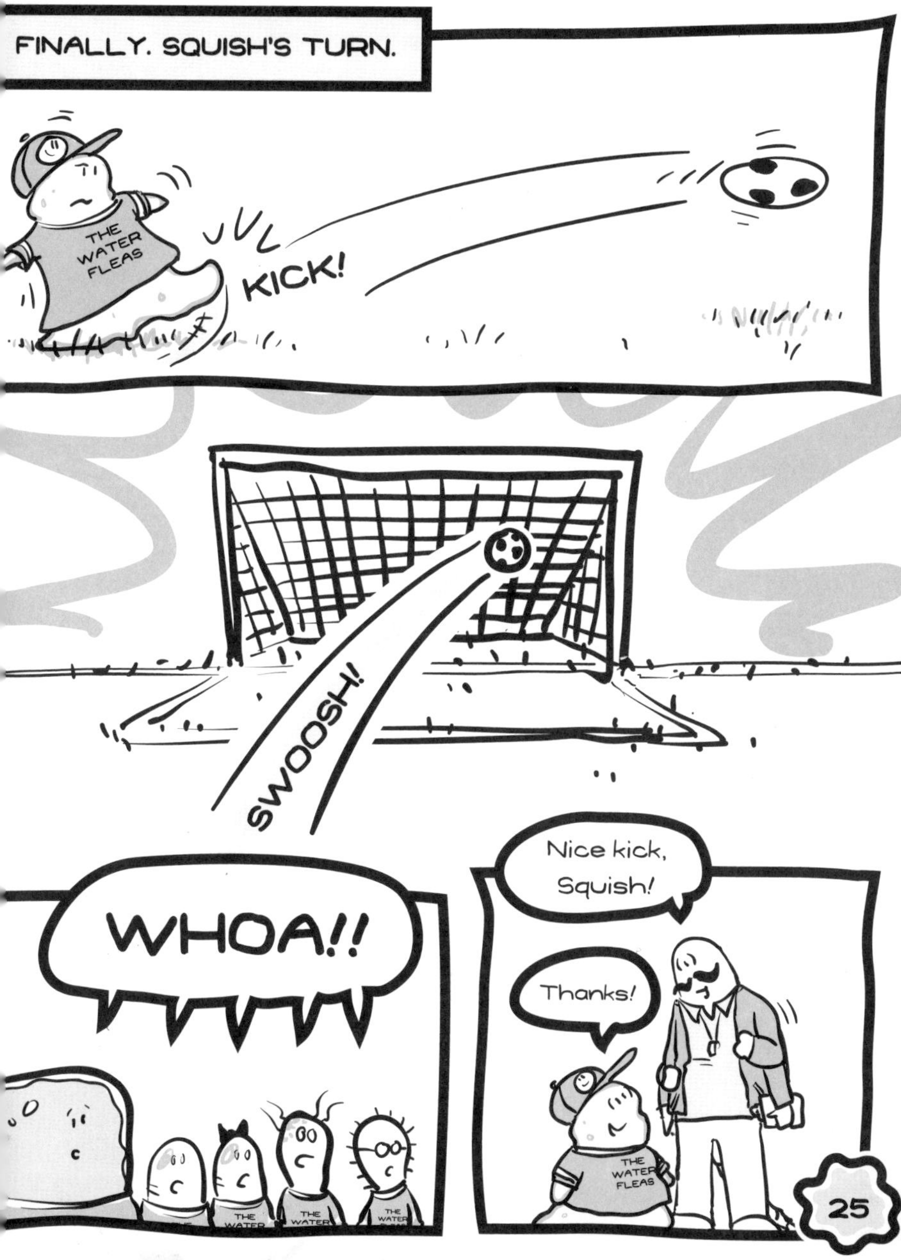
FINALLY. SQUISH'S TURN.
THE WATER FLEAS
KICK!
SWOOSH!
WHOA!!
Nice kick, Squish!
Thanks!
THE WATER FLEAS

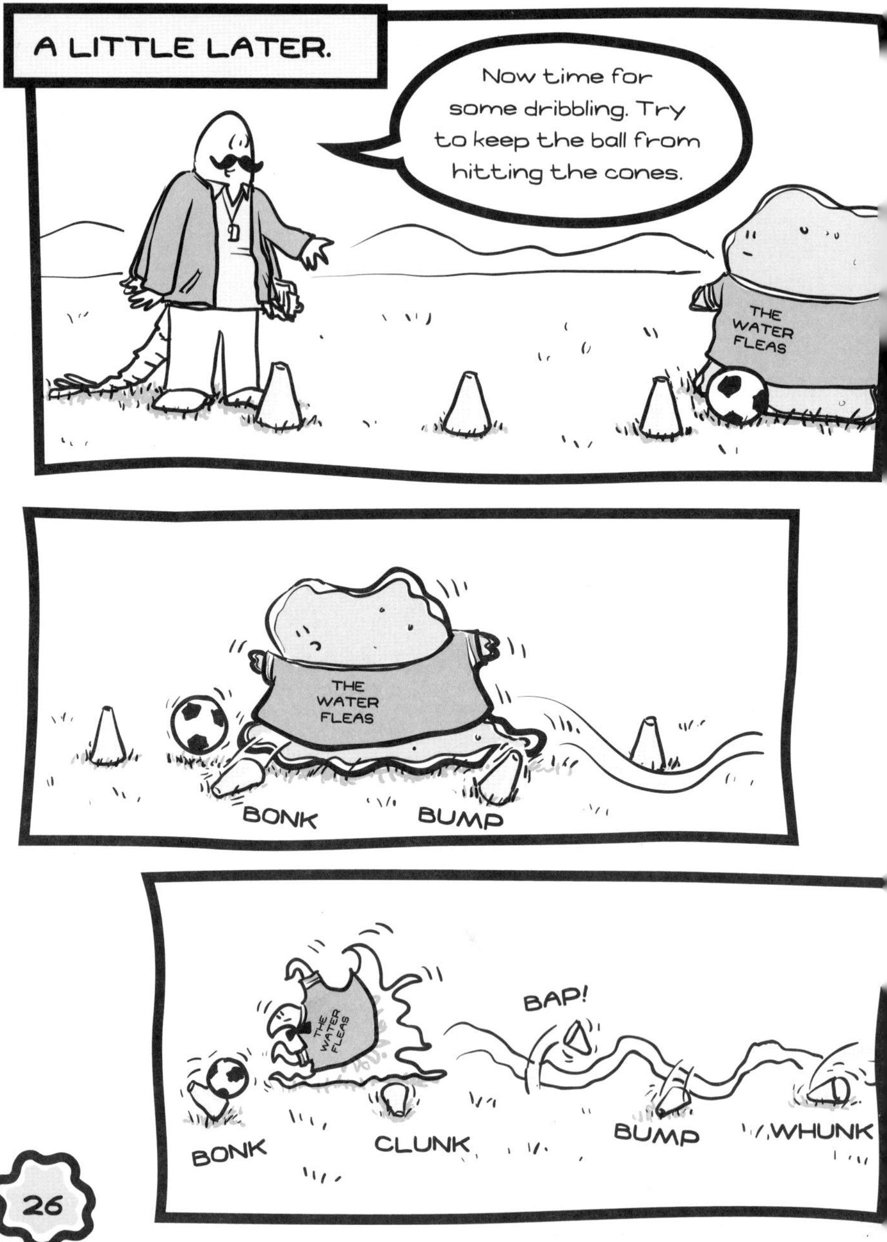
A LITTLE LATER.
Now time for some dribbling. Try to keep the ball from hitting the cones.
THE WATER FLEAS
THE WATER FLEAS
BONK
BUMP
THE WATER FLEAS
BAP!
BONK
CLUNK
BUMP
WHUNK

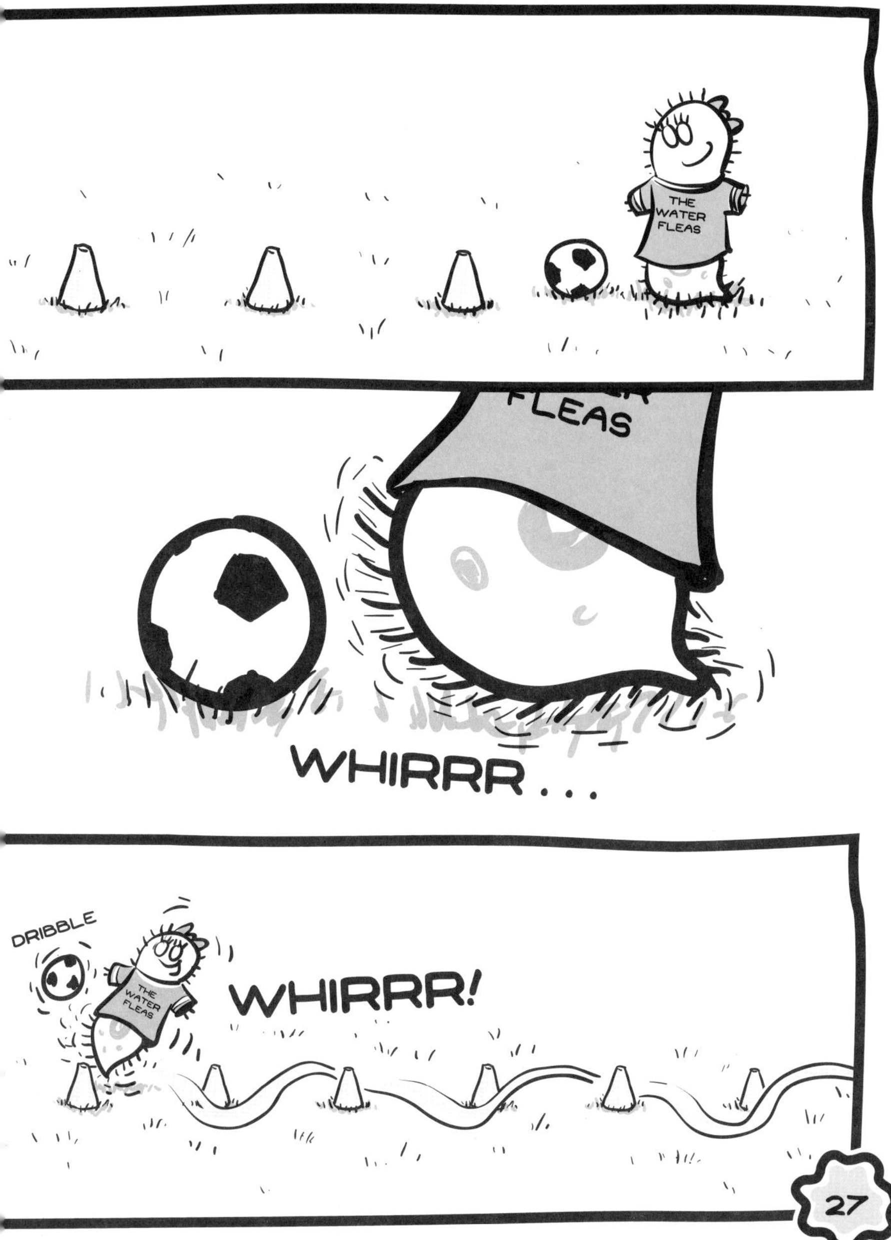
THE WATER FLEAS
FLEAS
WHIRRR . . .
DRIBBLE
THE WATER FLEAS
WHIRRR!

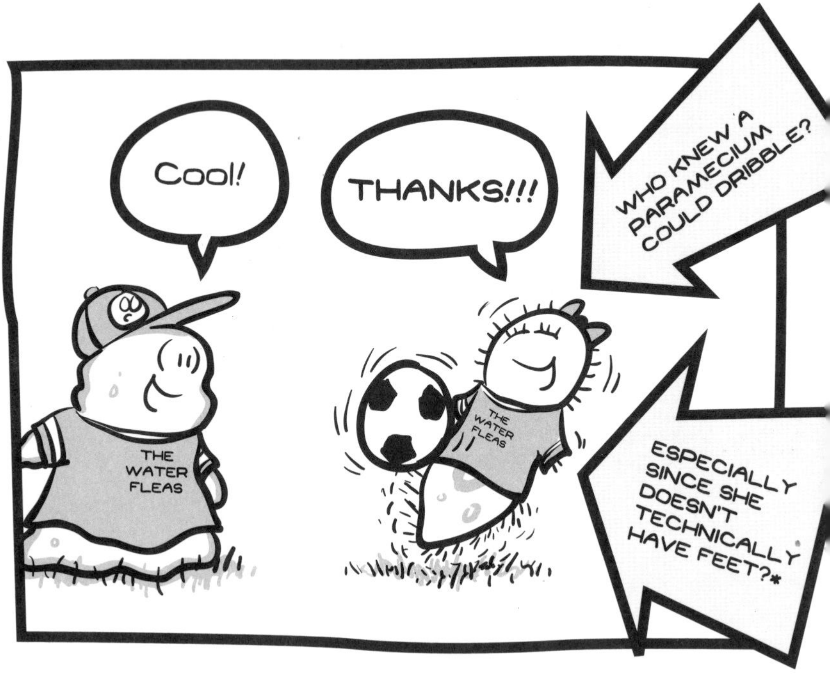
Cool!
THANKS!!!
THE WATER FLEAS
THE WATER FLEAS
WHO KNEW A PARAMECIUM COULD DRIBBLE?
ESPECIALLY SINCE SHE DOESN'T TECHNICALLY HAVE FEET?*

*CILIA ARE WHAT PARAMECIA HAVE INSTEAD OF HANDS AND FEET. SEE, YOU LEARNED SOMETHING!**
**TRY NOT TO MAKE A HABIT OF IT.

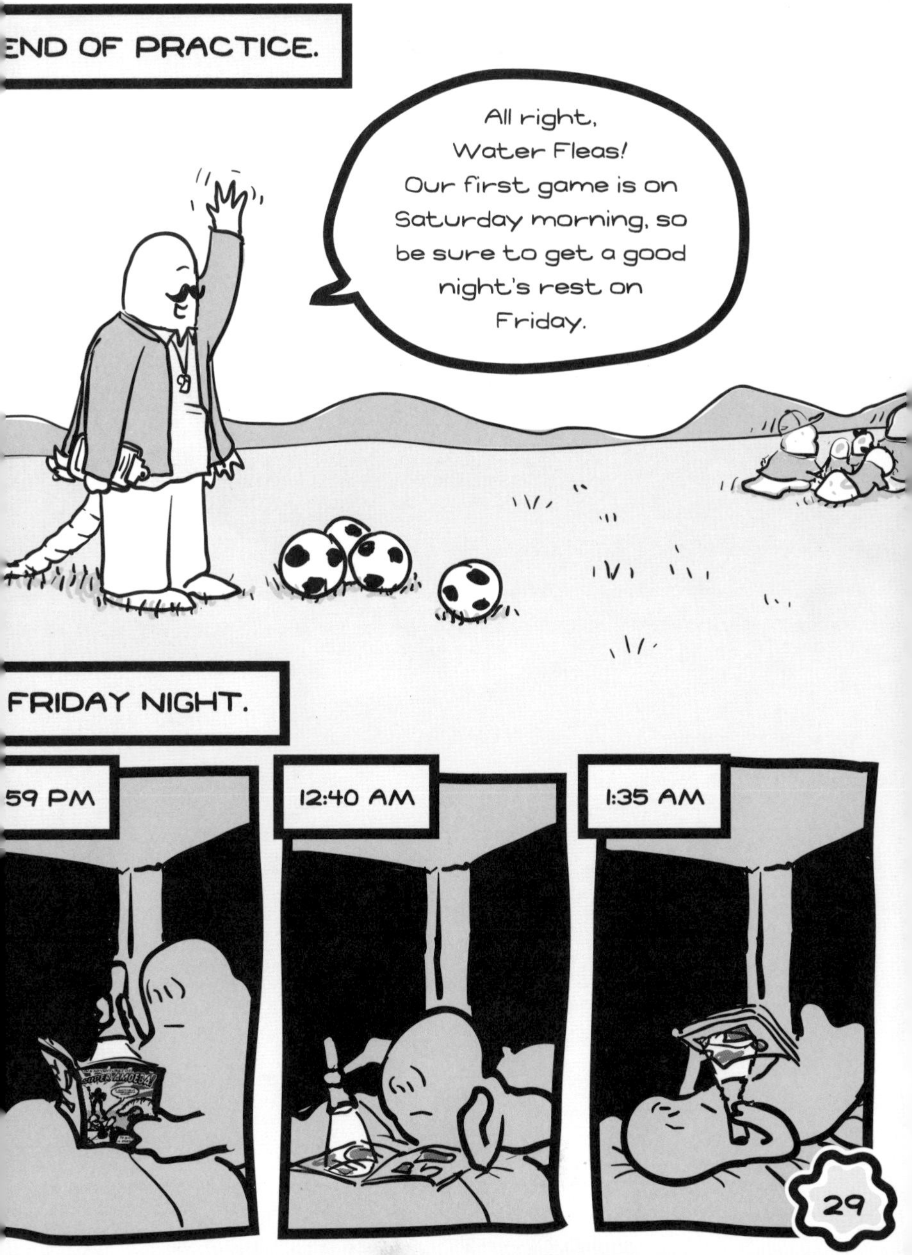

END OF PRACTICE.
All right, Water Fleas! Our first game is on Saturday morning, so be sure to get a good night's rest on Friday.
FRIDAY NIGHT.
59 PM
12:40 AM
1:35 AM

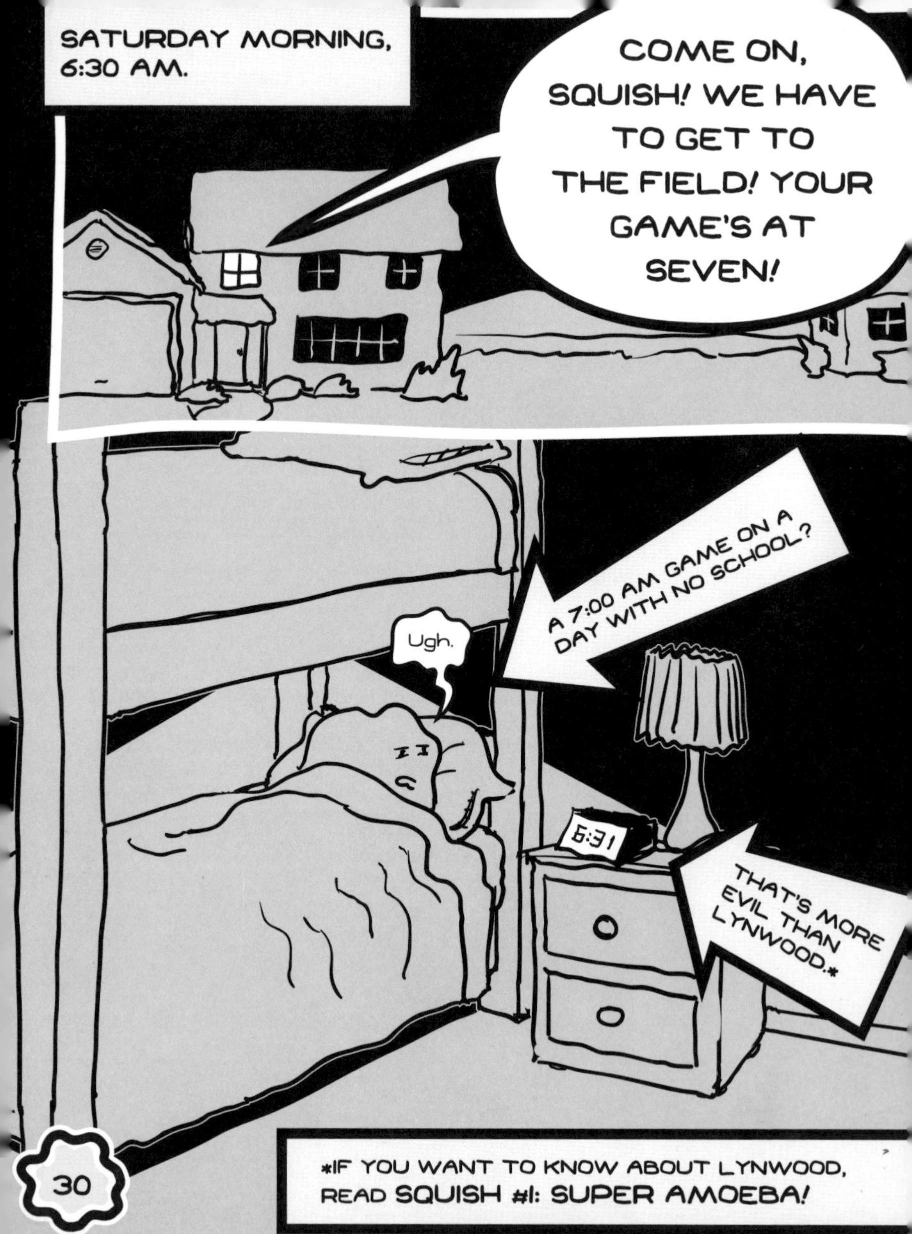
SATURDAY MORNING, 6:30 AM.
COME ON, SQUISH! WE HAVE TO GET TO THE FIELD! YOUR GAME'S AT SEVEN!
Ugh.
A 7:00 AM GAME ON A DAY WITH NO SCHOOL?
6:31
THAT'S MORE EVIL THAN LYNWOOD.*
*IF YOU WANT TO KNOW ABOUT LYNWOOD, READ SQUISH #1: SUPER AMOEBA!

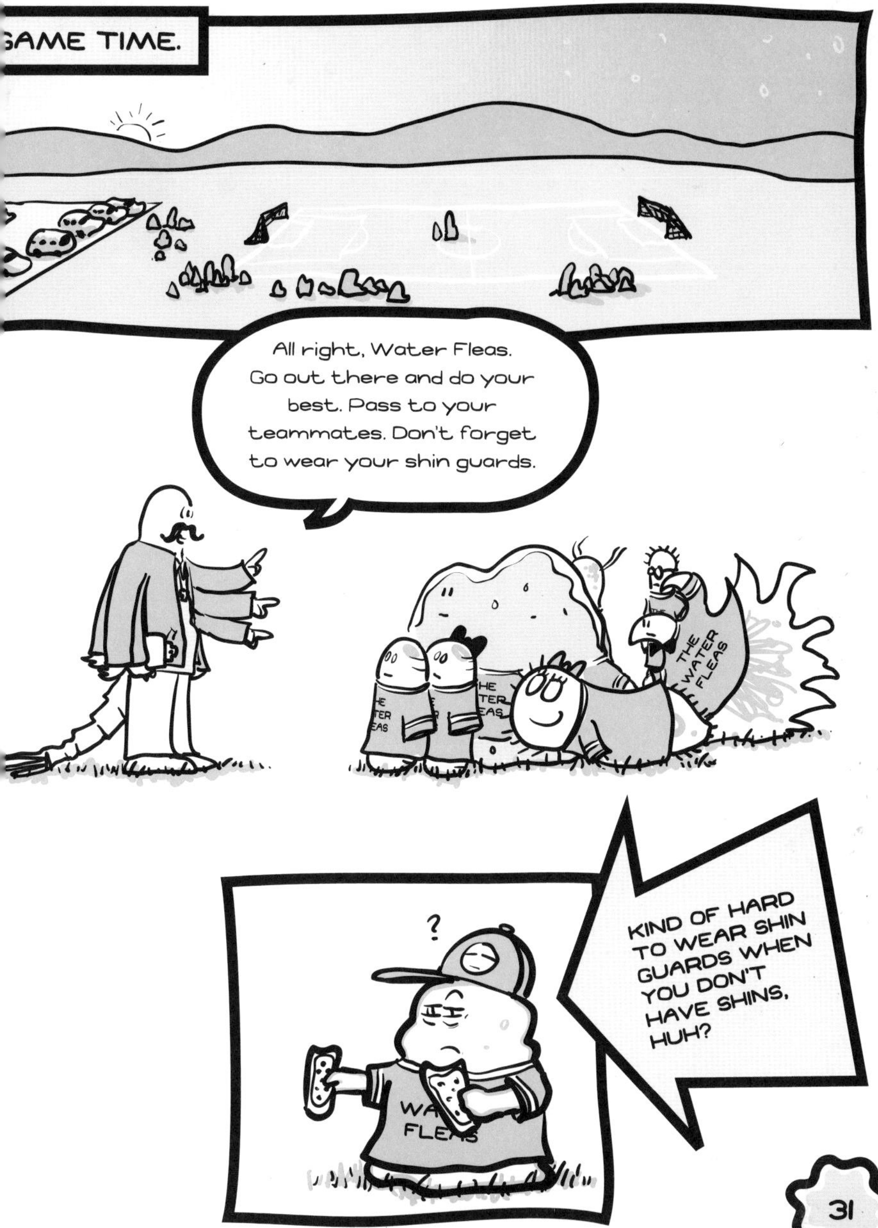
GAME TIME.
All right, Water Fleas. Go out there and do your best. Pass to your teammates. Don't forget to wear your shin guards.
THE WATER FLEAS
?
KIND OF HARD TO WEAR SHIN GUARDS WHEN YOU DON'T HAVE SHINS, HUH?
FLEAS

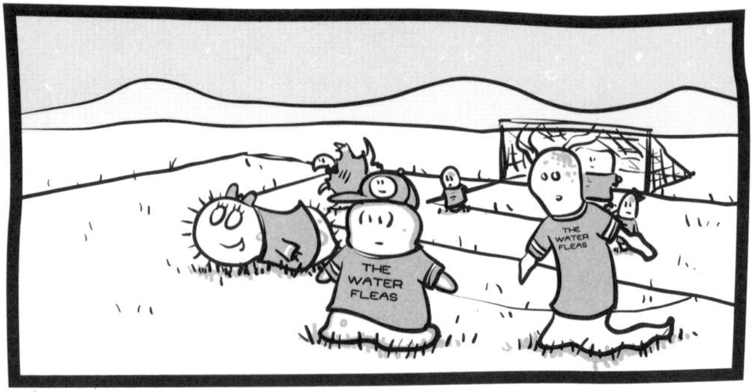
THE WATER FLEAS
THE WATER FLEAS

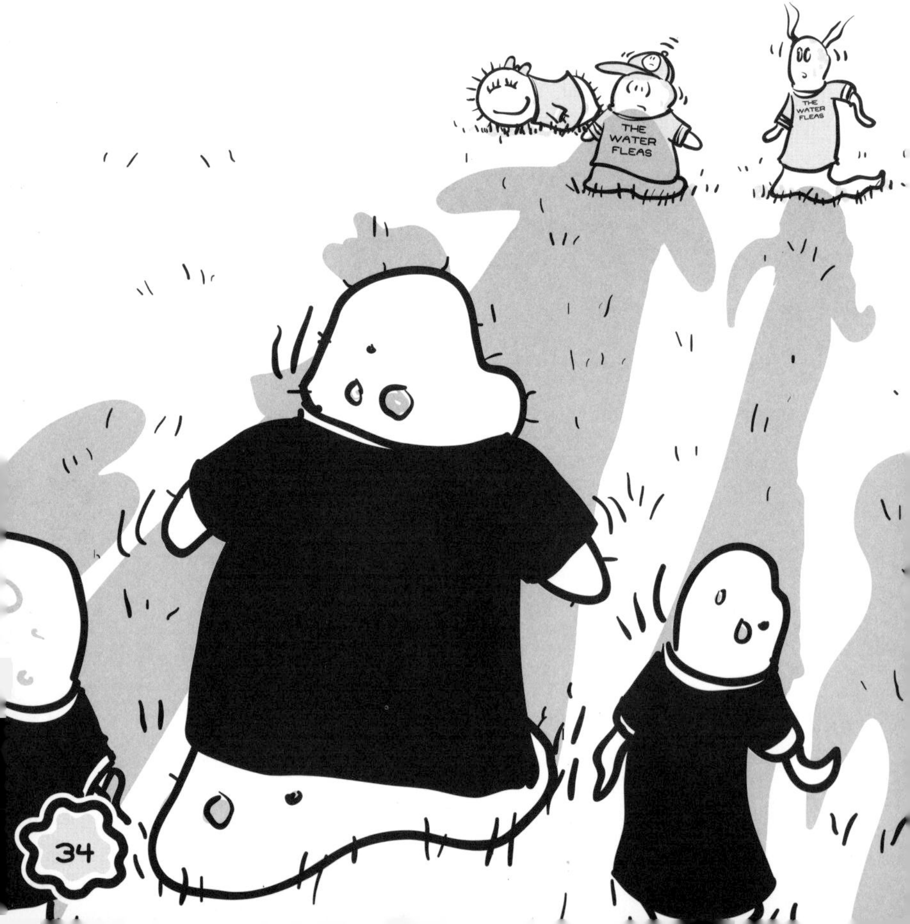
THE WATER FLEAS
THE WATER FLEAS

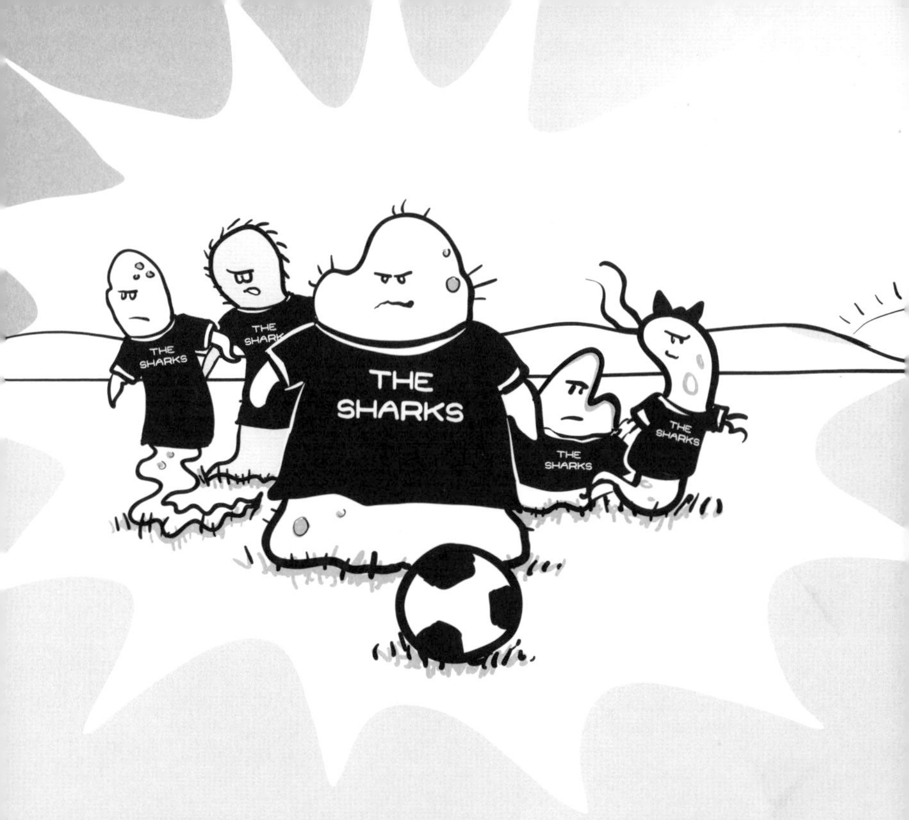
THE SHARKS
THE SHARKS
THE SHARKS
THE SHARKS
THE SHARKS

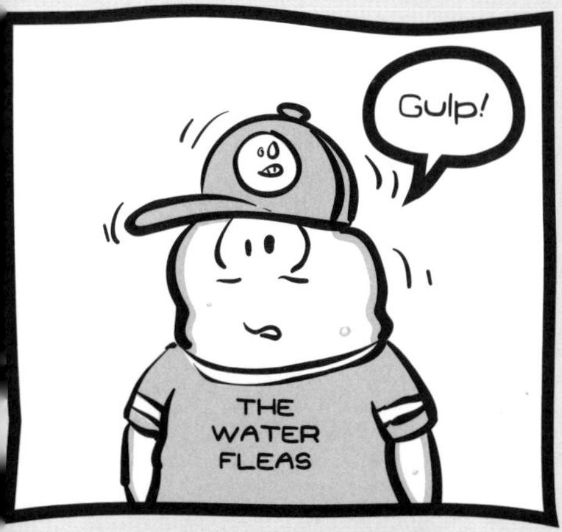
Gulp!
THE WATER FLEAS

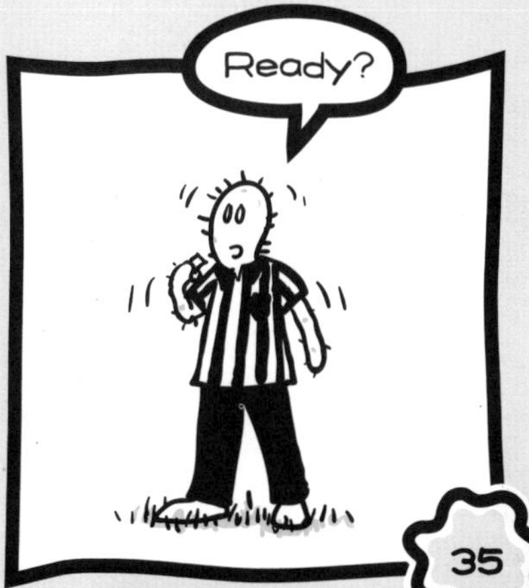
Ready?

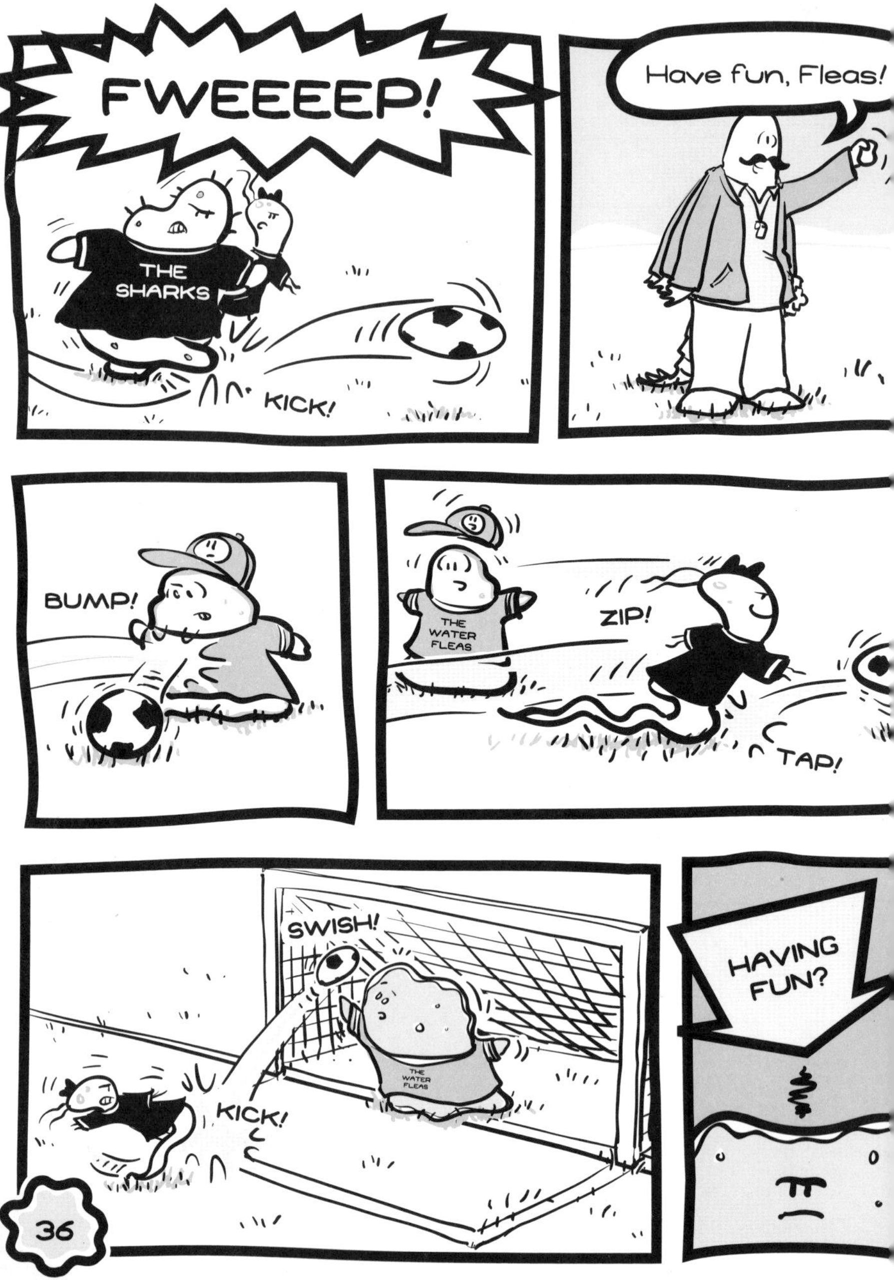
FWEEEEP!
THE SHARKS
KICK!
Have fun, Fleas!
BUMP!
THE WATER FLEAS
ZIP!
TAP!
SWISH!
THE WATER FLEAS
KICK!
HAVING FUN?

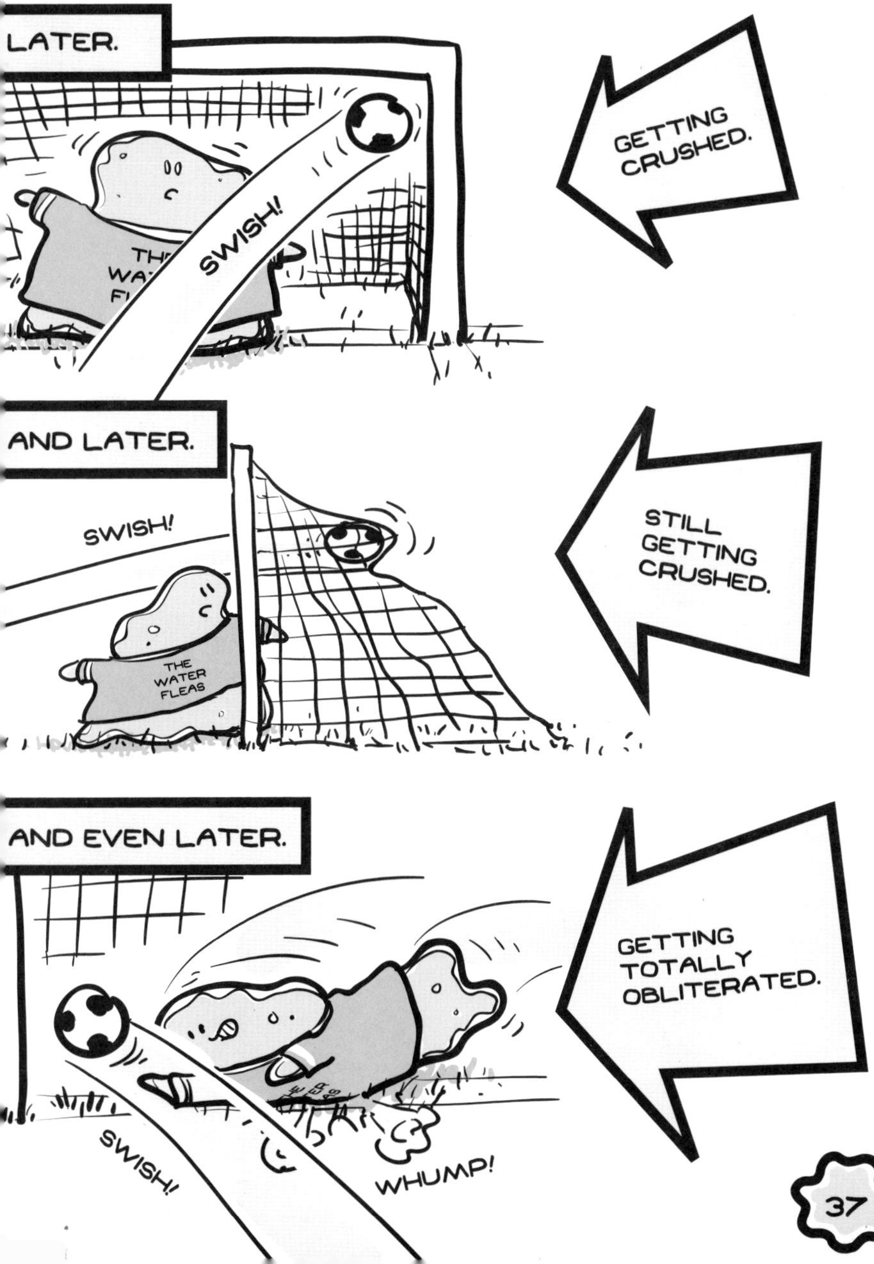
LATER.
SWISH!
GETTING CRUSHED.
AND LATER.
SWISH!
THE WATER FLEAS
STILL GETTING CRUSHED.
AND EVEN LATER.
SWISH!
WHUMP!
GETTING TOTALLY OBLITERATED.

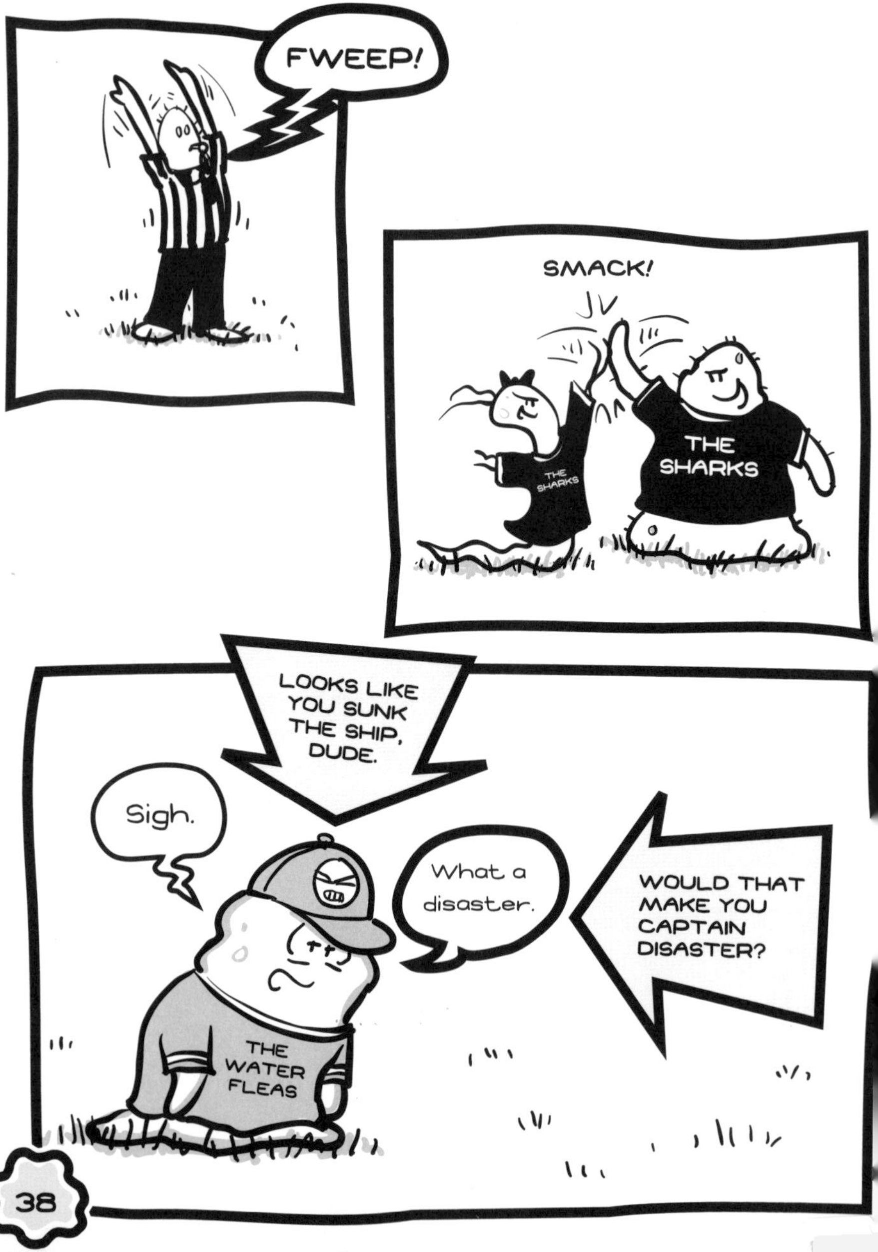
FWEEP!
SMACK!
THE SHARKS
THE SHARKS
LOOKS LIKE YOU SUNK THE SHIP, DUDE.
Sigh.
What a disaster.
WOULD THAT MAKE YOU CAPTAIN DISASTER?
THE WATER FLEAS

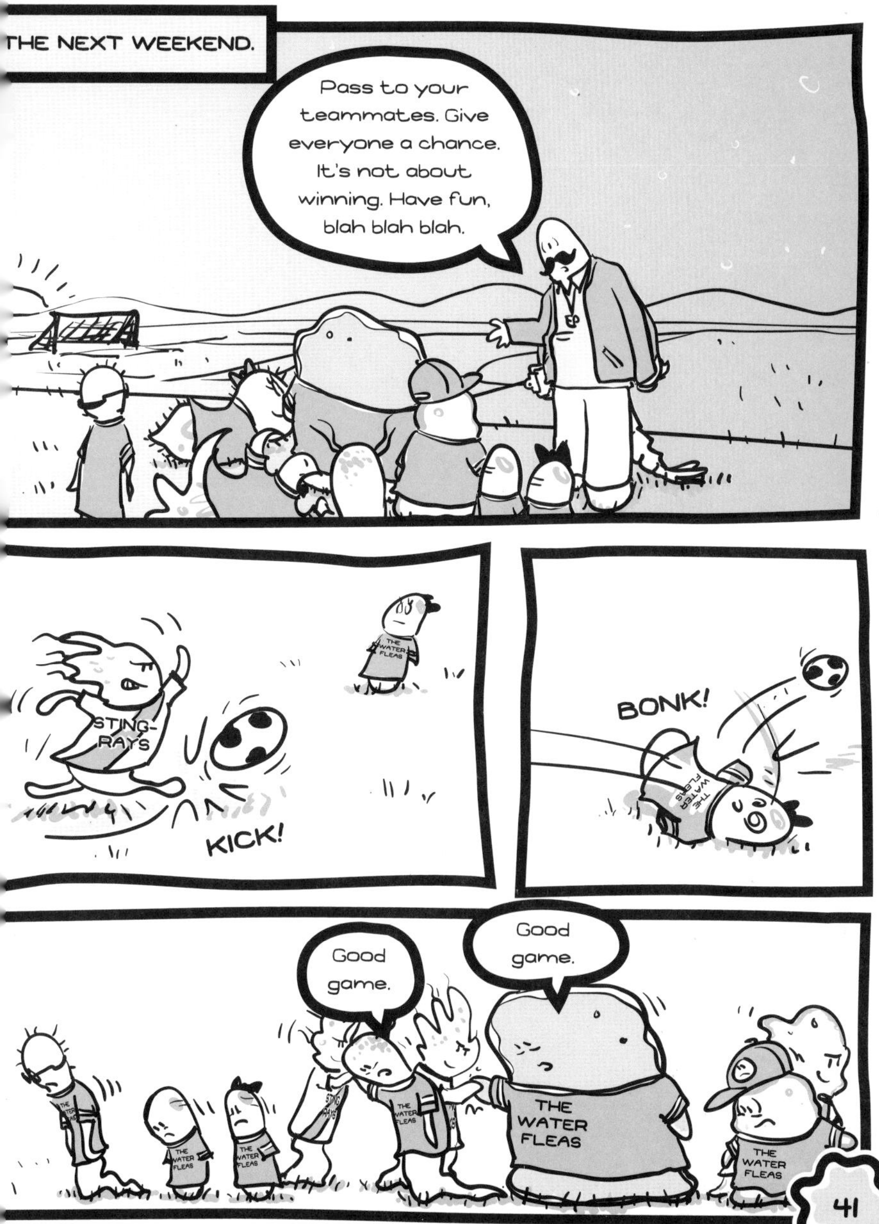
THE NEXT WEEKEND.
Pass to your teammates. Give everyone a chance. It's not about winning. Have fun, blah blah blah.
THE WATER FLEAS
STING-RAYS
KICK!
BONK!
THE WATER FLEAS
Good game.
Good game.
THE WATER FLEAS
THE WATER FLEAS
THE WATER FLEAS
THE WATER FLEAS
THE WATER FLEAS

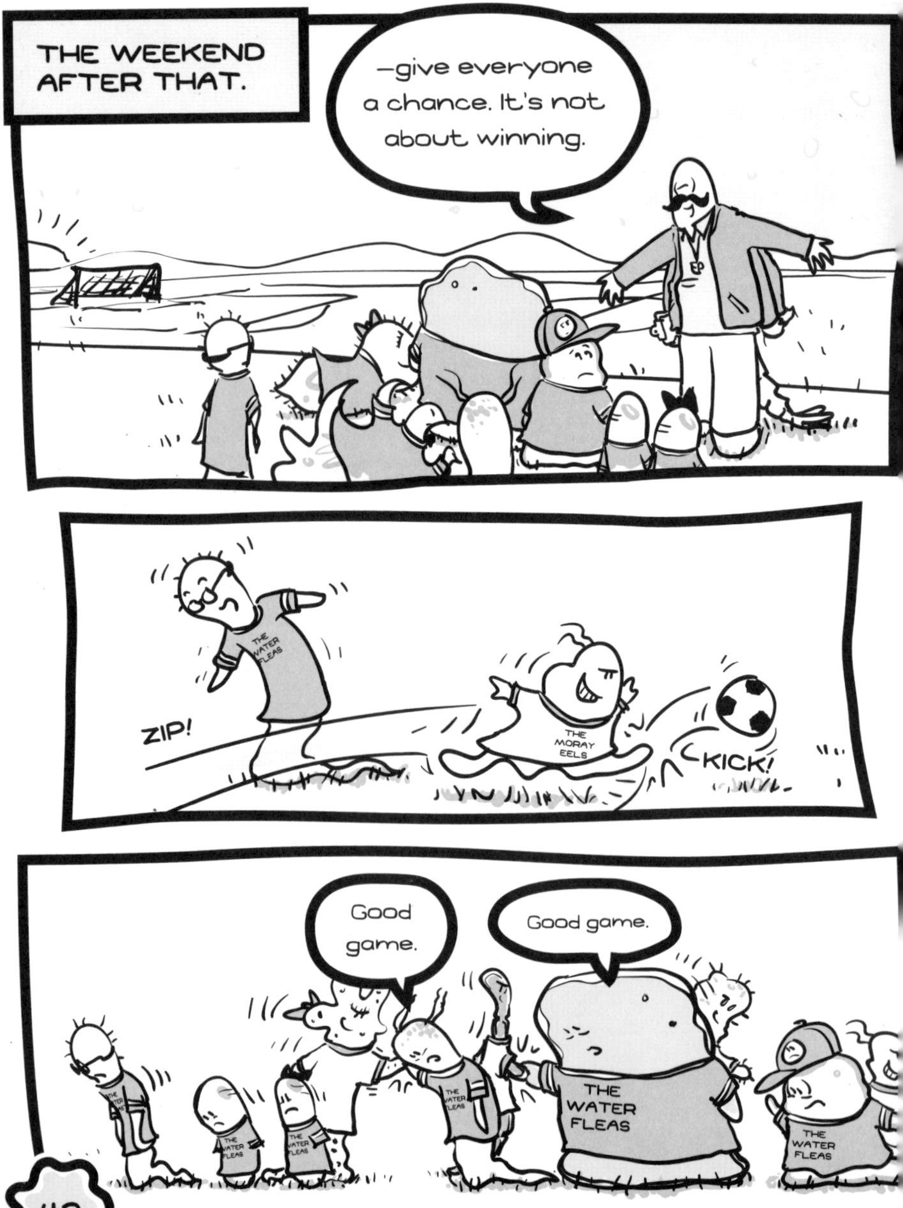
THE WEEKEND AFTER THAT.
—give everyone a chance. It's not about winning.
THE WATER FLEAS
ZIP!
THE MORAY EELS
KICK!
Good game.
Good game.
THE WATER FLEAS
THE WATER FLEAS
THE WATER FLEAS
THE WATER FLEAS

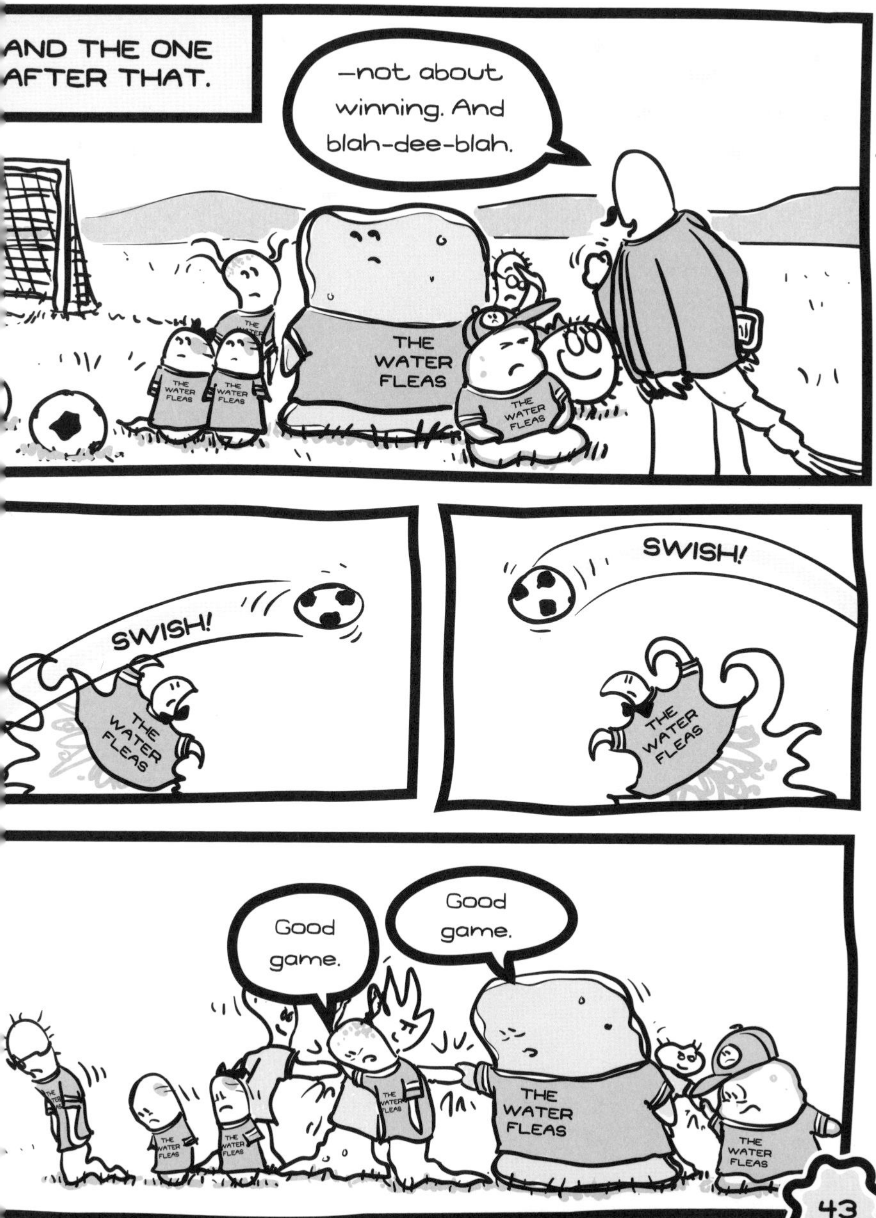
AND THE ONE AFTER THAT.
—not about winning. And blah-dee-blah.
THE WATER FLEAS
SWISH!
THE WATER FLEAS
SWISH!
THE WATER FLEAS
Good game.
Good game.
THE WATER FLEAS
THE WATER FLEAS

THAT NIGHT.

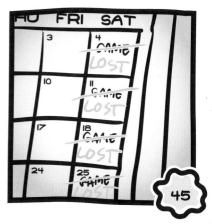

45

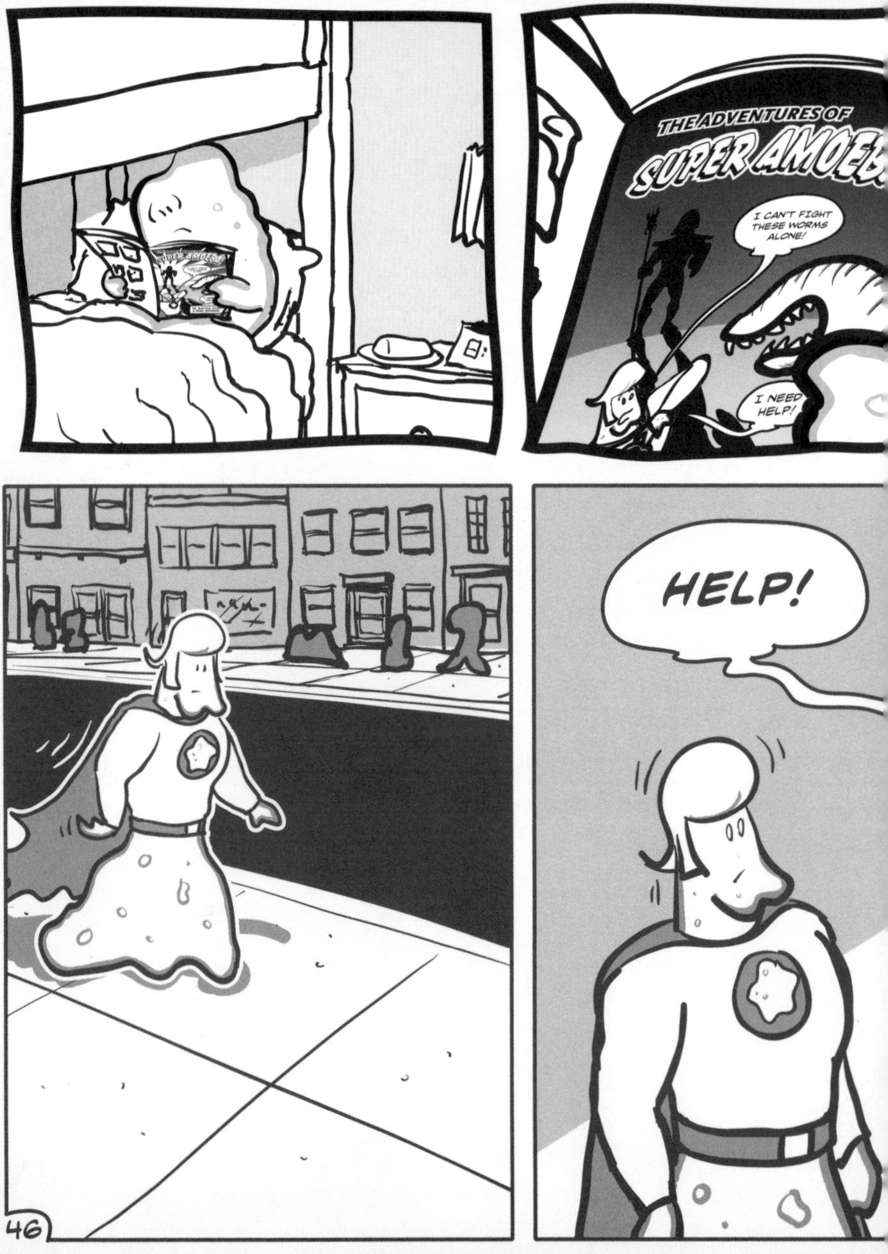
THE ADVENTURES OF
SUPER AMOEB
I CAN'T FIGHT THESE WORMS ALONE!
I NEED HELP!
HELP!

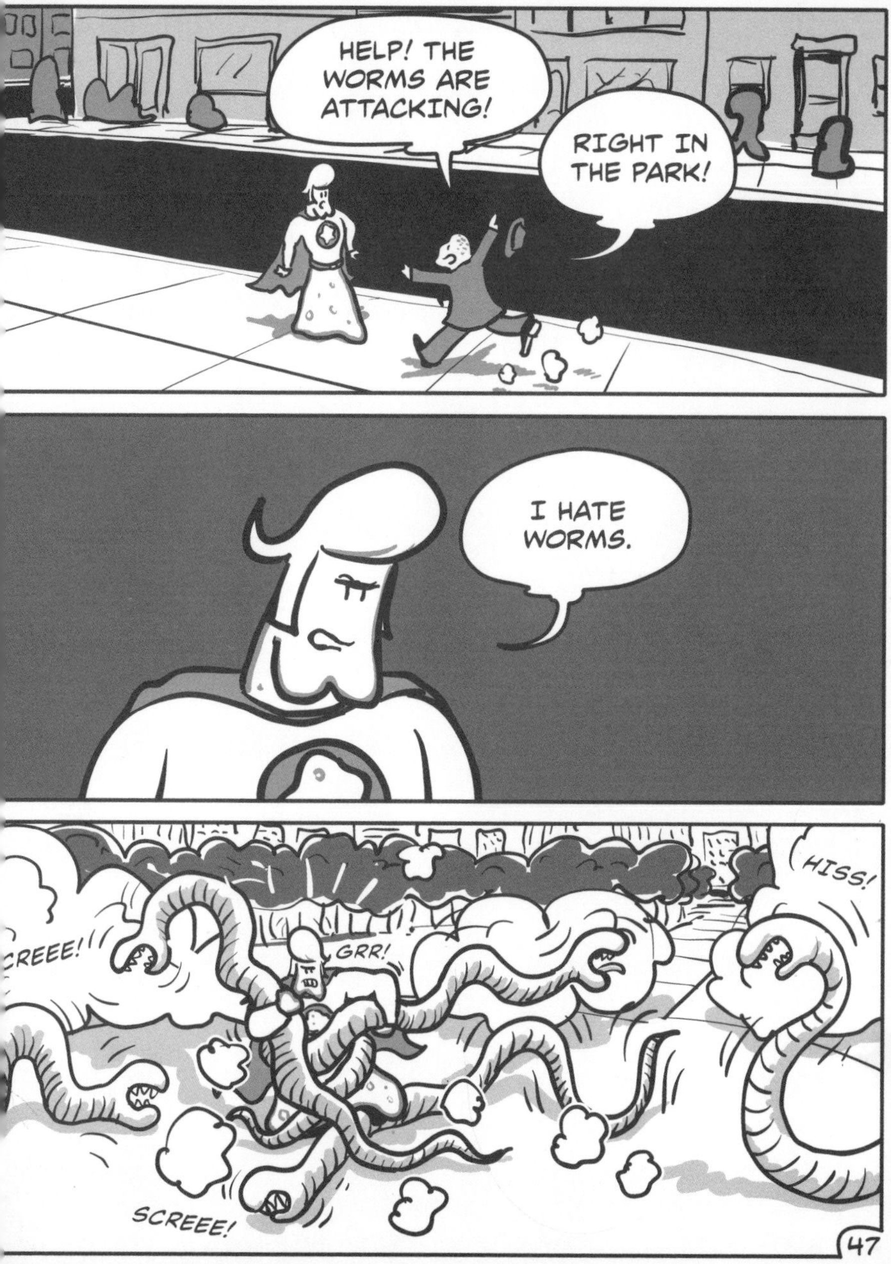
HELP! THE WORMS ARE ATTACKING!
RIGHT IN THE PARK!
I HATE WORMS.
CREEE!
GRR!
HISS!
SCREEE!

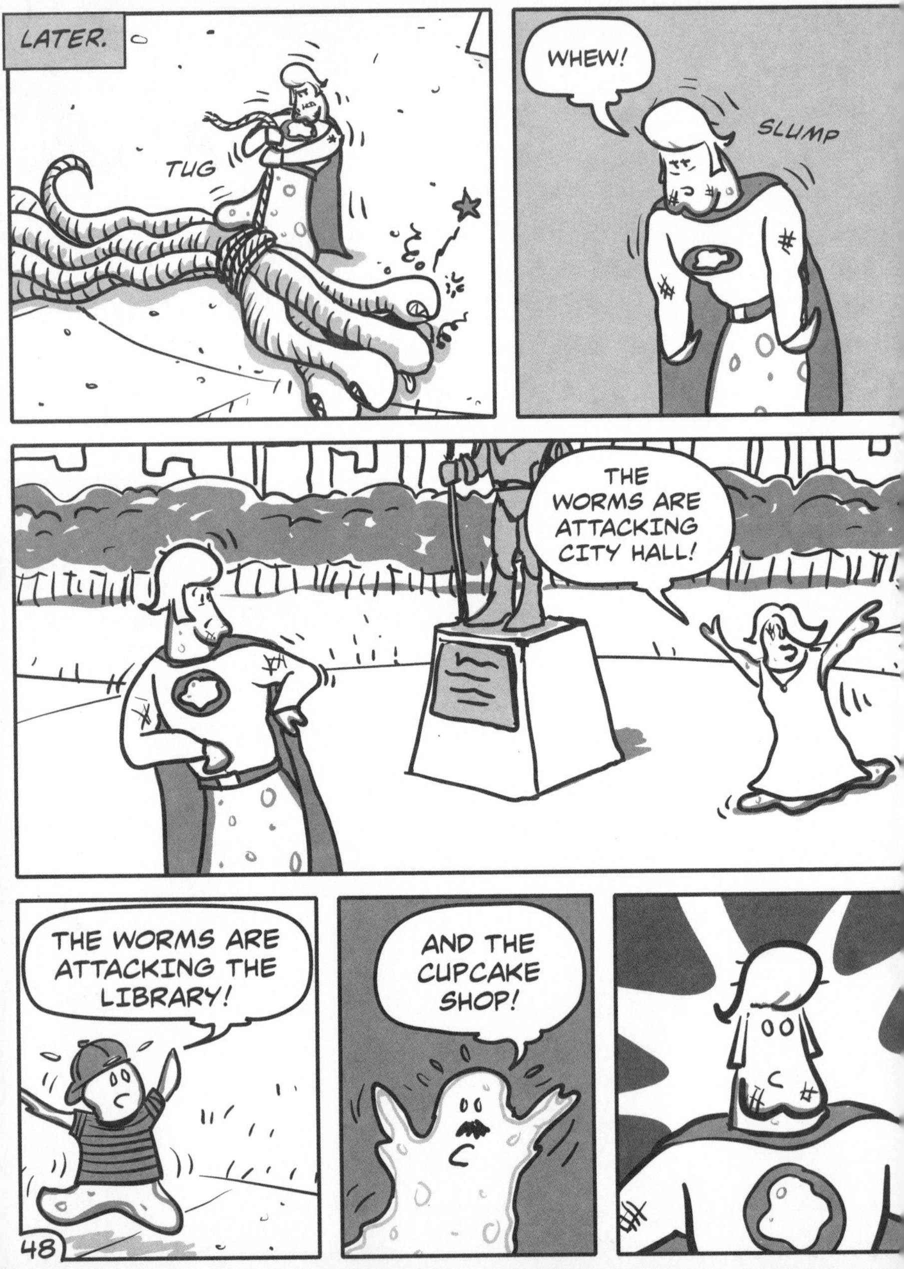
LATER.
TUG
WHEW!
SLUMP
THE WORMS ARE ATTACKING CITY HALL!
THE WORMS ARE ATTACKING THE LIBRARY!
AND THE CUPCAKE SHOP!

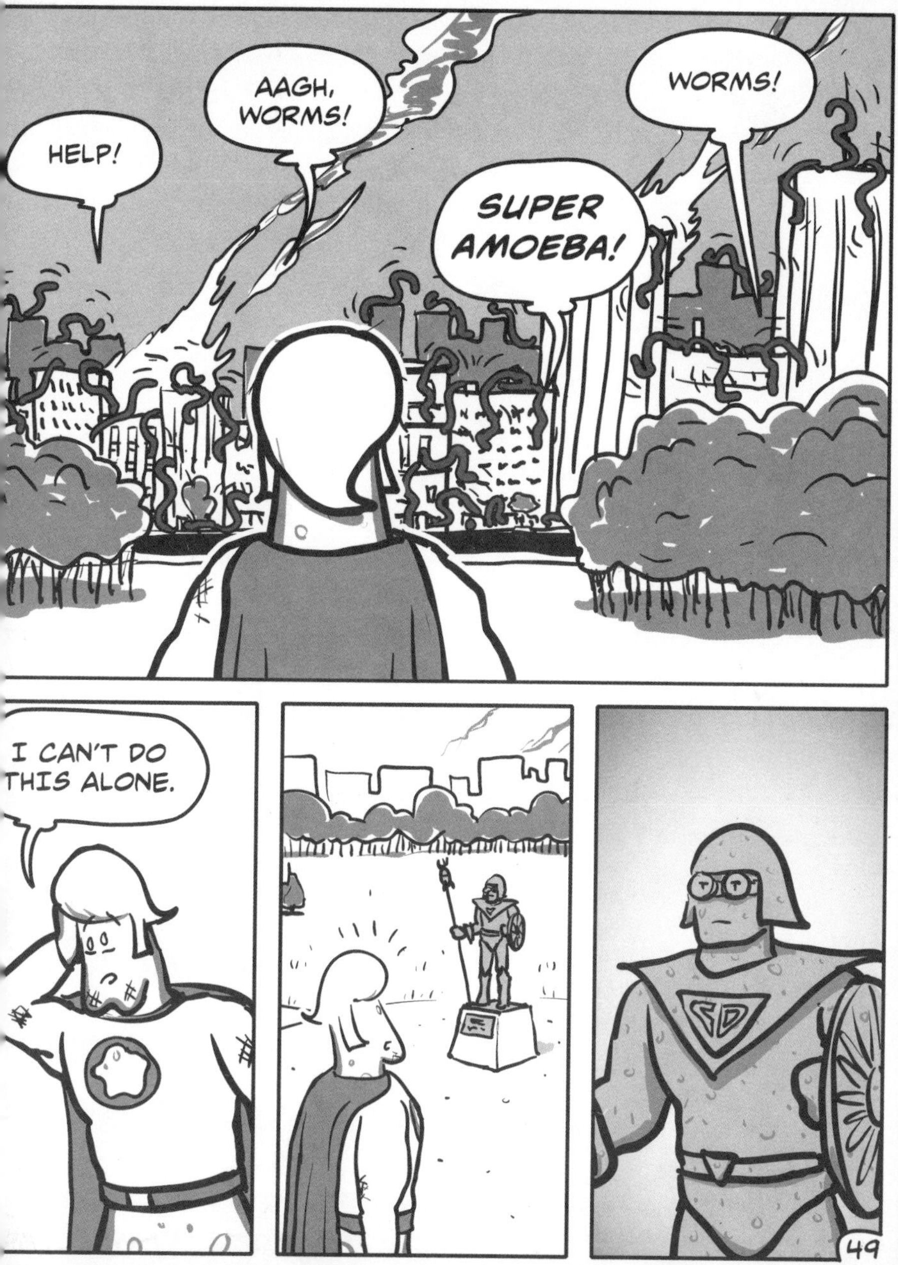
HELP!
AAGH, WORMS!
SUPER AMOEBA!
WORMS!
I CAN'T DO THIS ALONE.

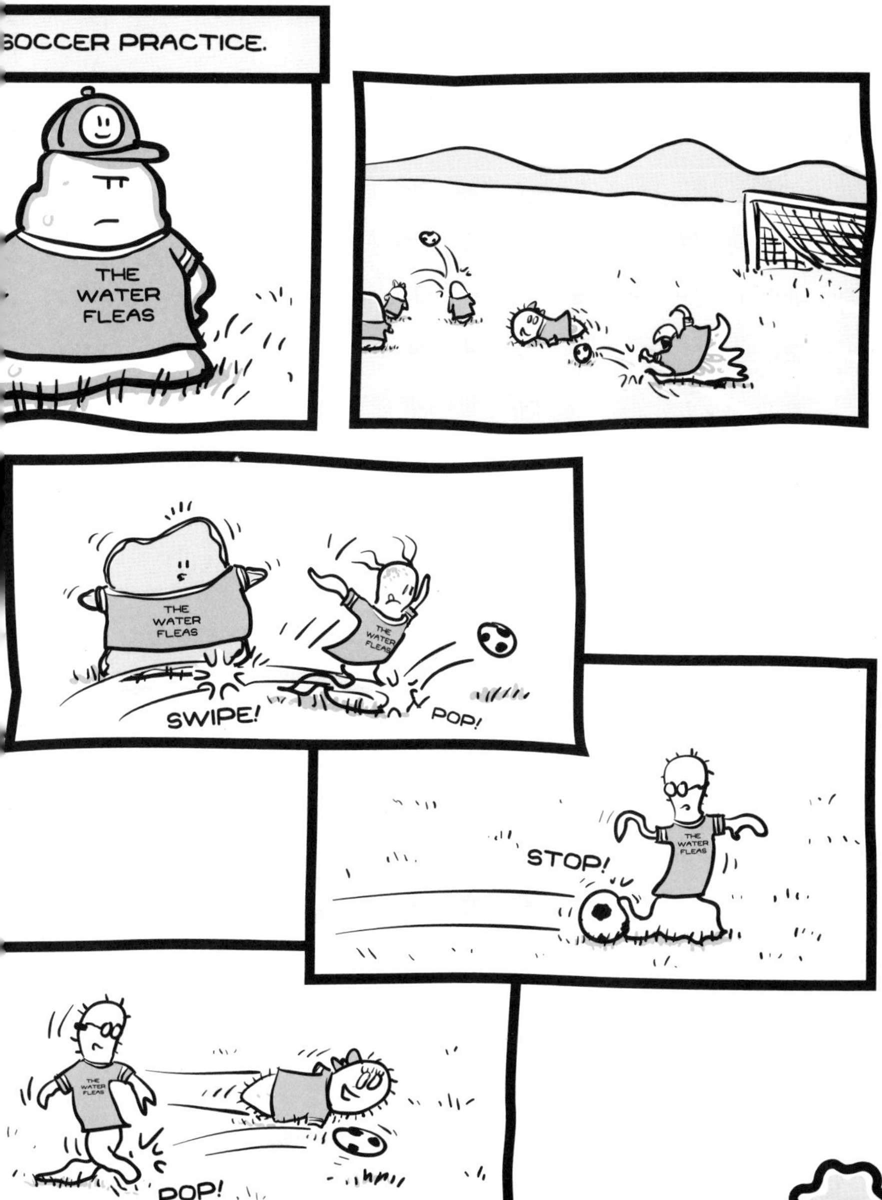
SOCCER PRACTICE.
THE WATER FLEAS
THE WATER FLEAS
THE WATER FLEAS
SWIPE!
POP!
STOP!
THE WATER FLEAS
THE WATER FLEAS
POP!

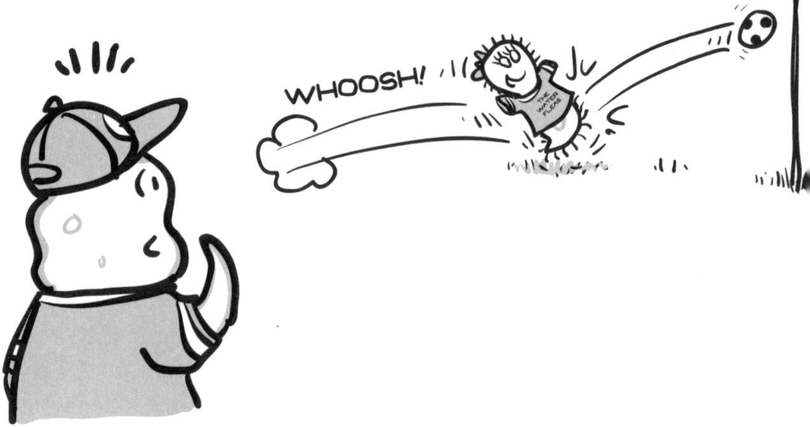
WHOOSH!
THE WATER FLEAS

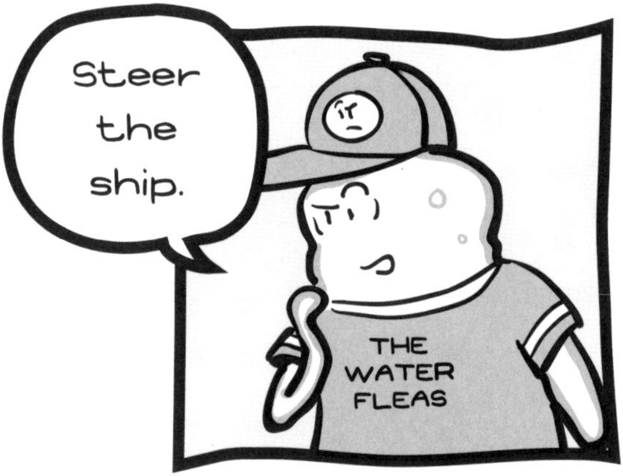
Steer the ship.
THE WATER FLEAS

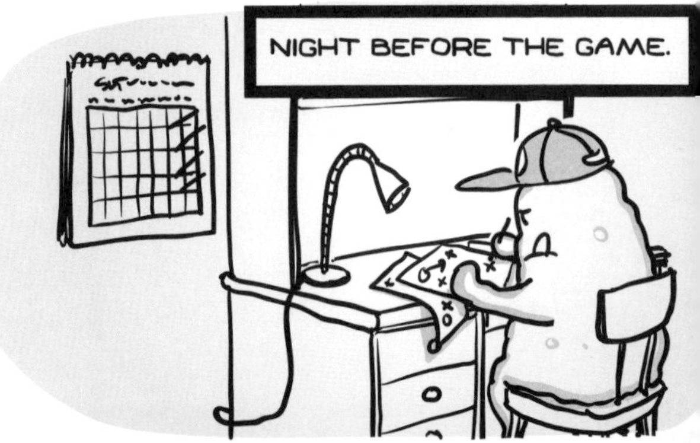
NIGHT BEFORE THE GAME.

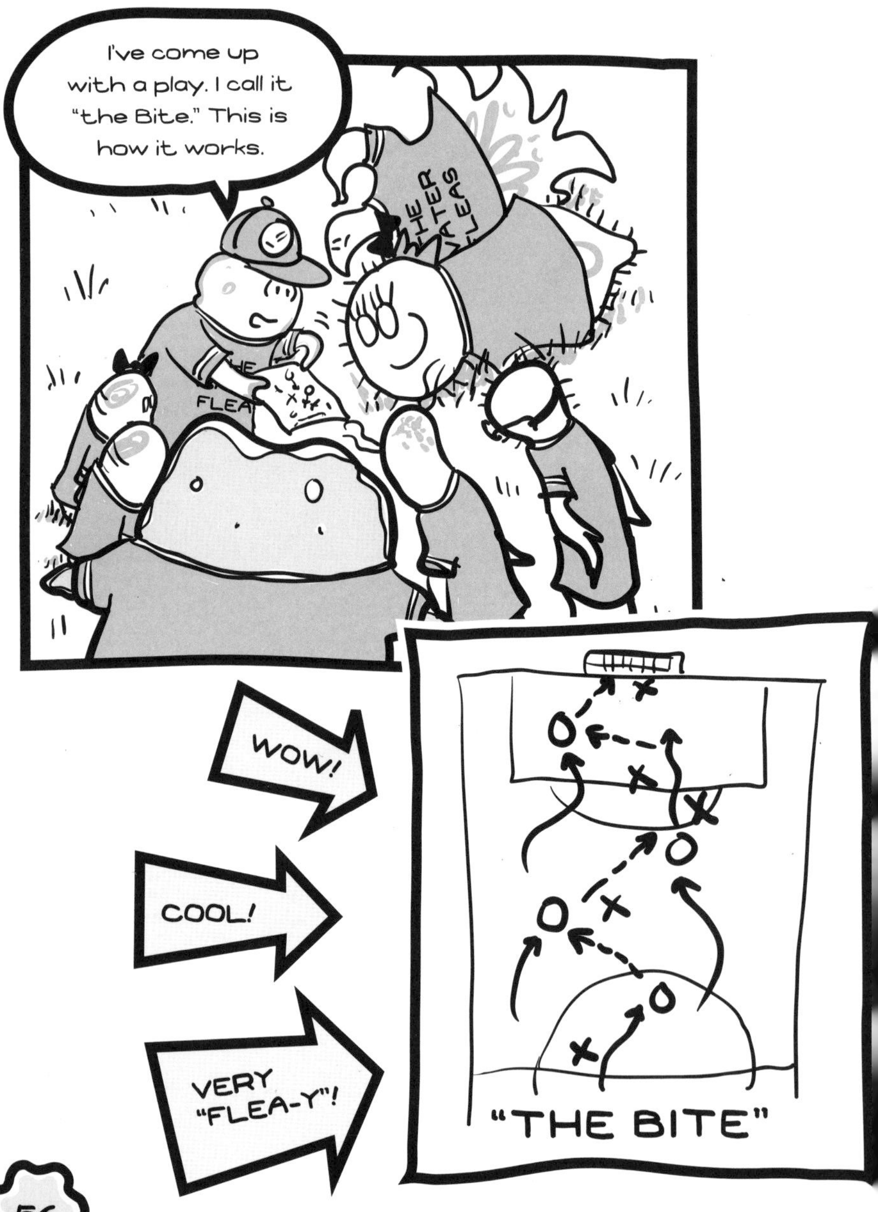

I've come up with a play. I call it "the Bite." This is how it works.
THE OTTER WATER FLEAS
FLEA
WOW!
COOL!
VERY "FLEA-Y"!
"THE BITE"

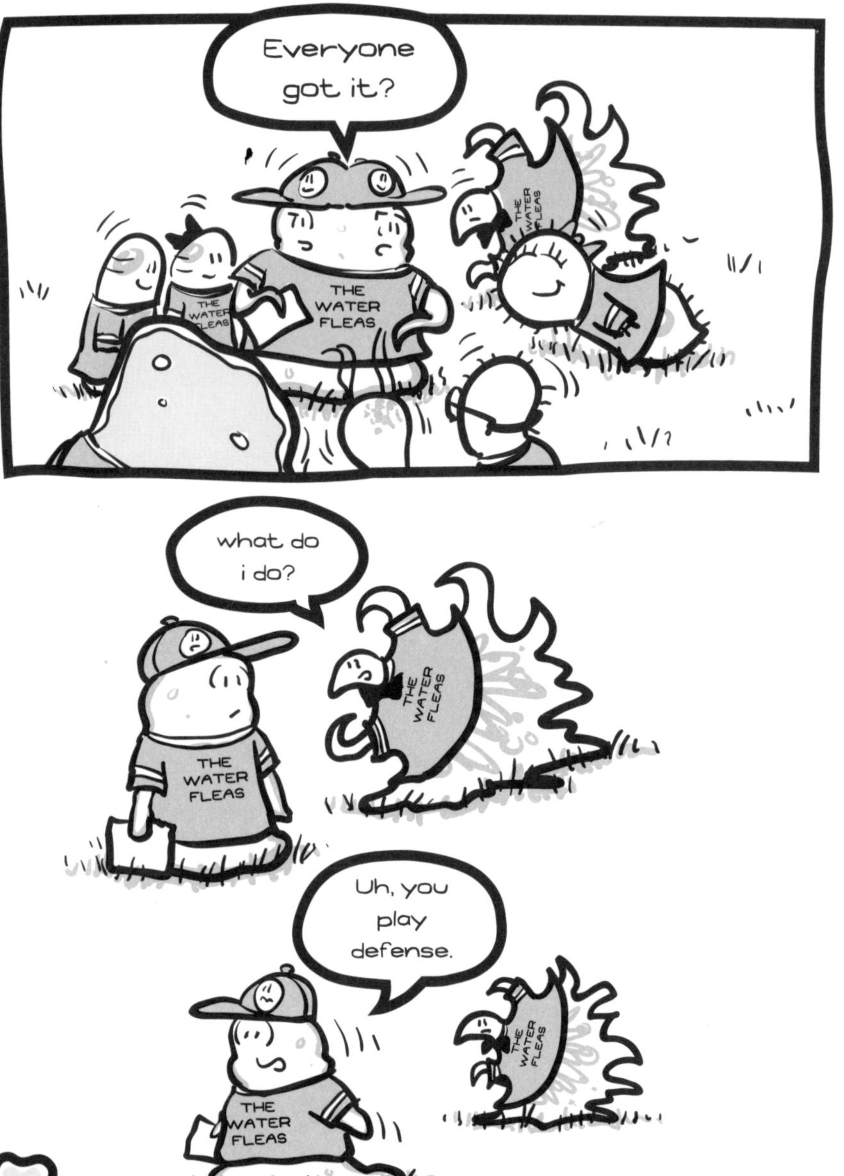
Everyone got it?
THE WATER FLEAS
what do i do?
Uh, you play defense.

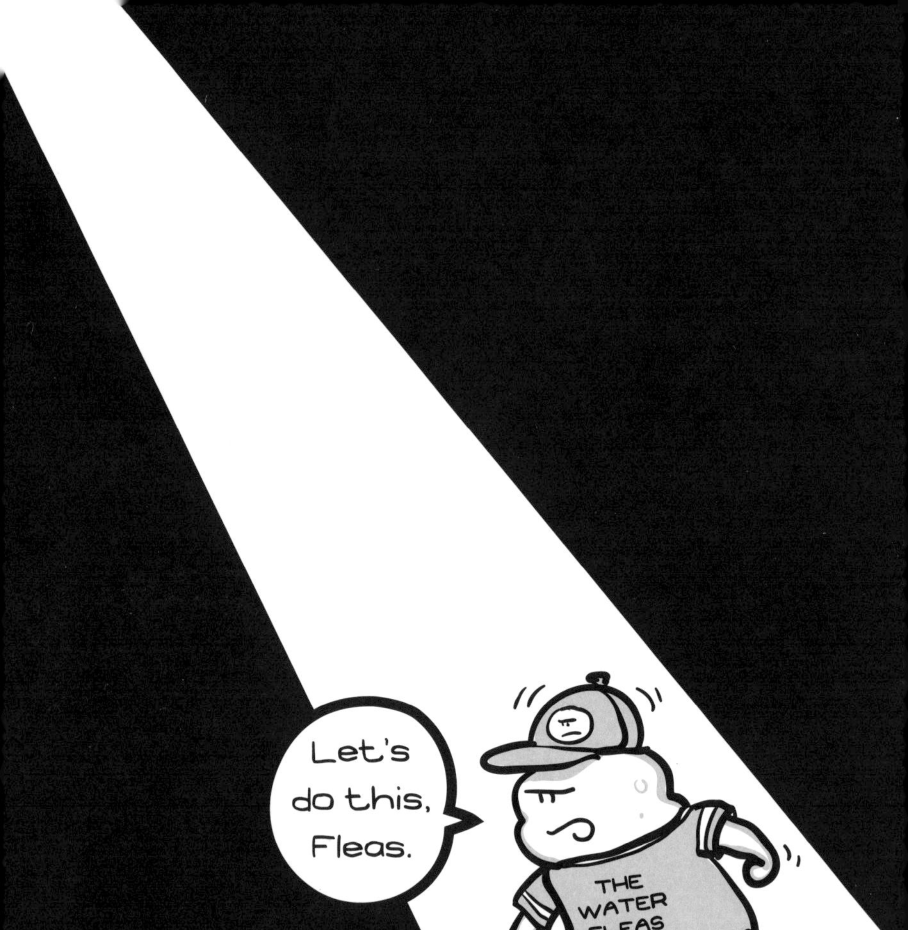
Let's do this, Fleas.
THE WATER FLEAS

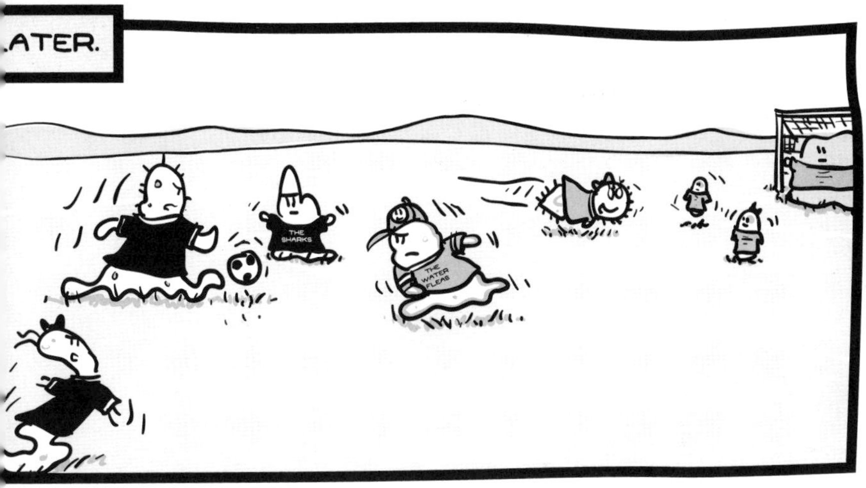

...LATER.
THE SHARKS
THE WATER FLEAS

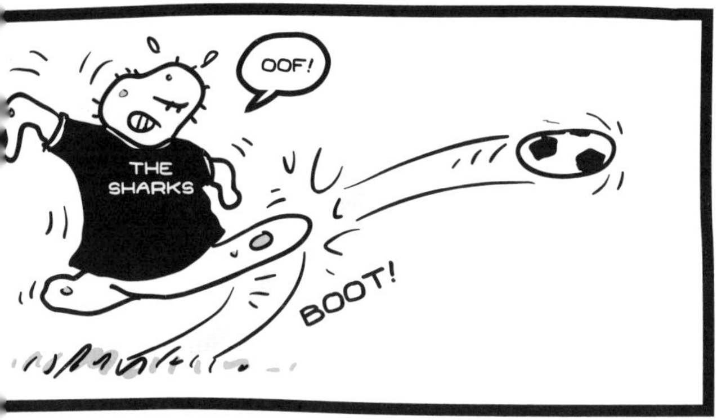

OOF!
THE SHARKS
BOOT!

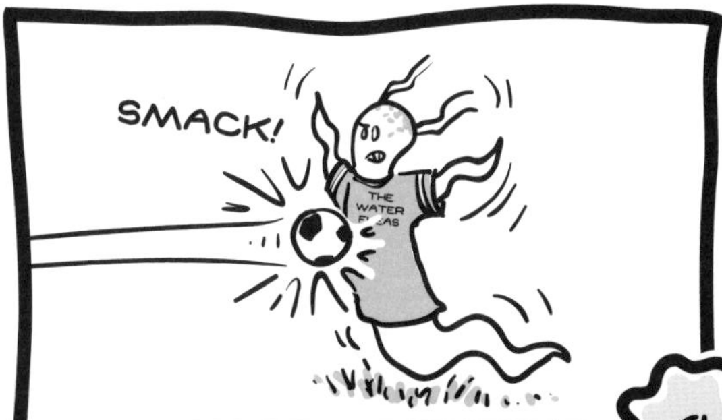

SMACK!
THE WATER FLEAS

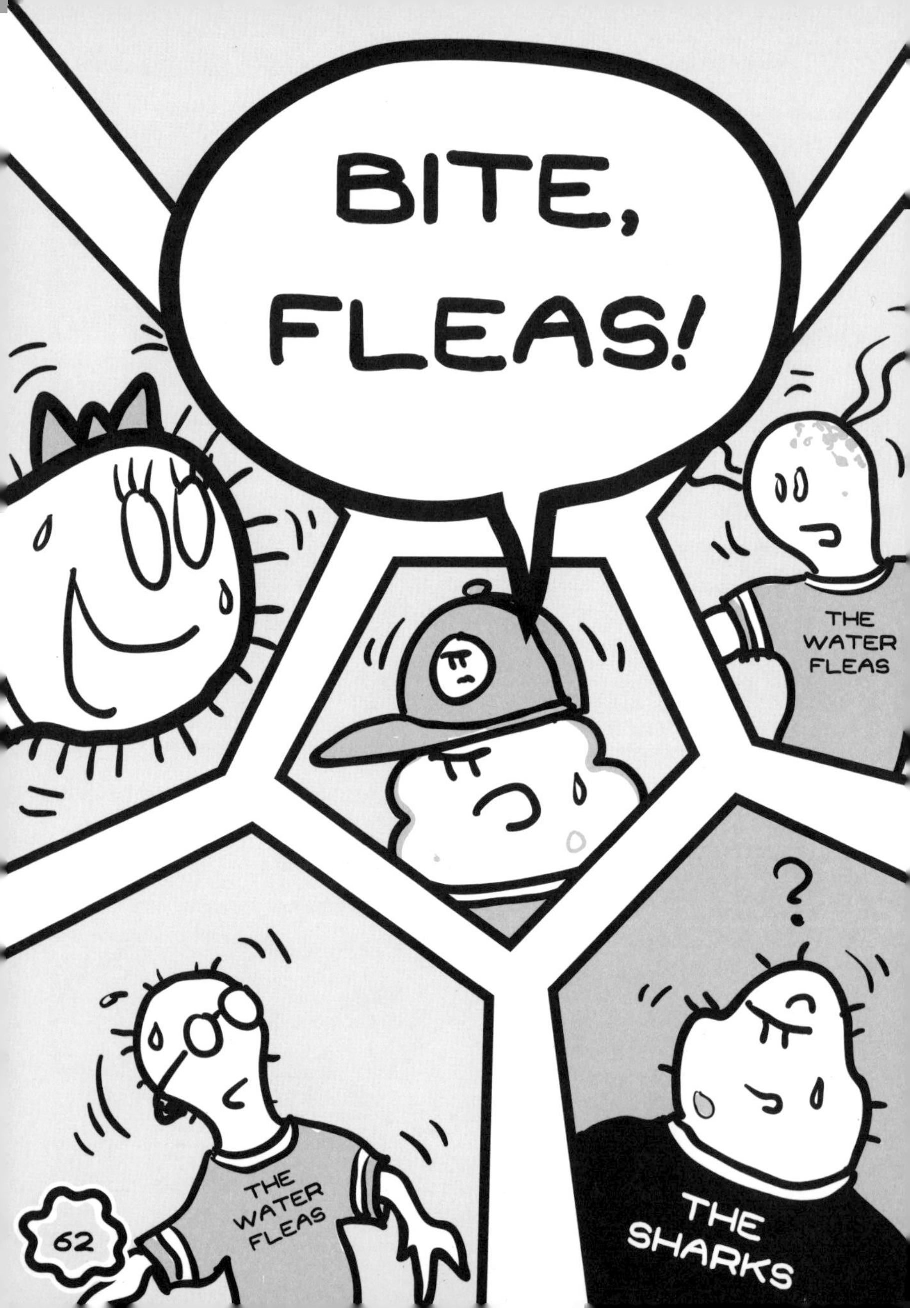
BITE, FLEAS!
THE WATER FLEAS
THE WATER FLEAS
THE SHARKS

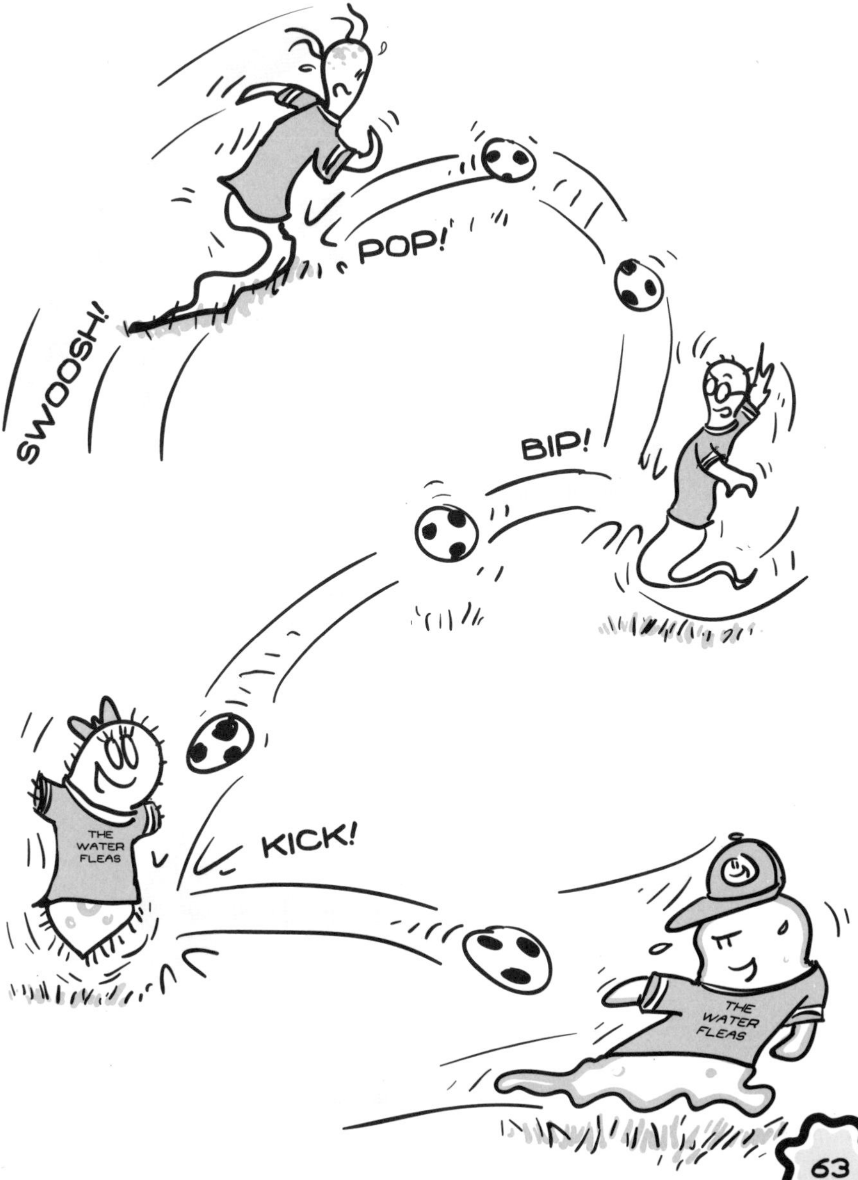
SWOOSH!
POP!
BIP!
KICK!
THE WATER FLEAS
THE WATER FLEAS

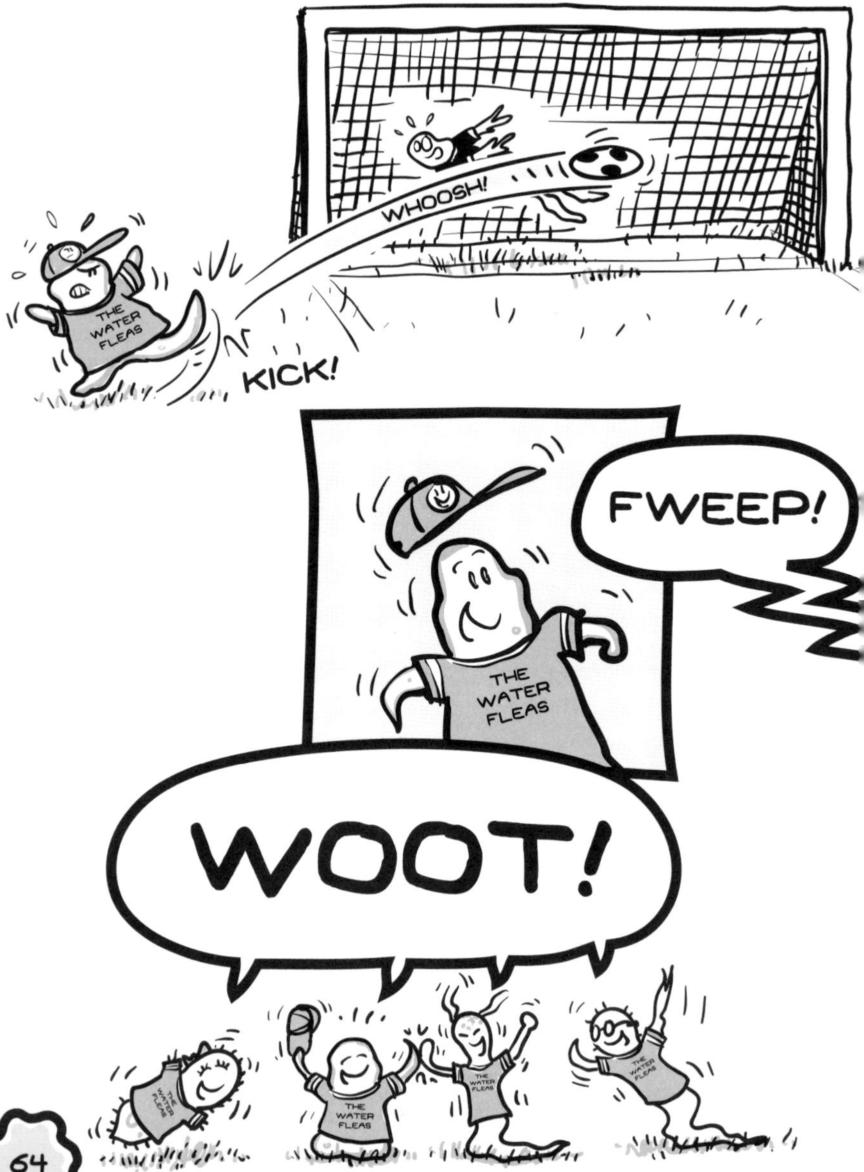
THE WATER FLEAS
WHOOSH!
KICK!
THE WATER FLEAS
FWEEP!
WOOT!
THE WATER FLEAS
THE WATER FLEAS
THE WATER FLEAS
THE WATER FLEAS

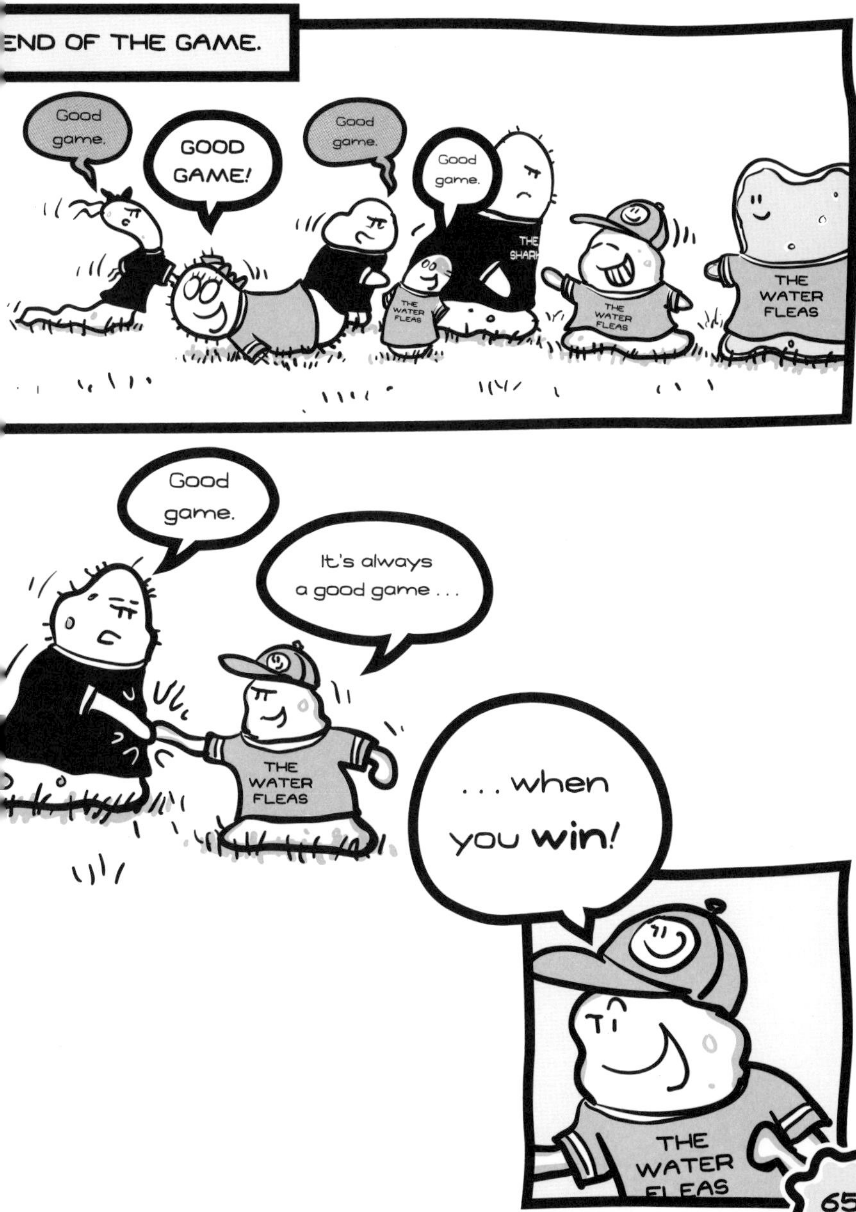
END OF THE GAME.
Good game.
GOOD GAME!
Good game.
Good game.
THE SHARK
THE WATER FLEAS
THE WATER FLEAS
THE WATER FLEAS
Good game.
It's always a good game . . .
THE WATER FLEAS
. . . when you win!
THE WATER FLEAS

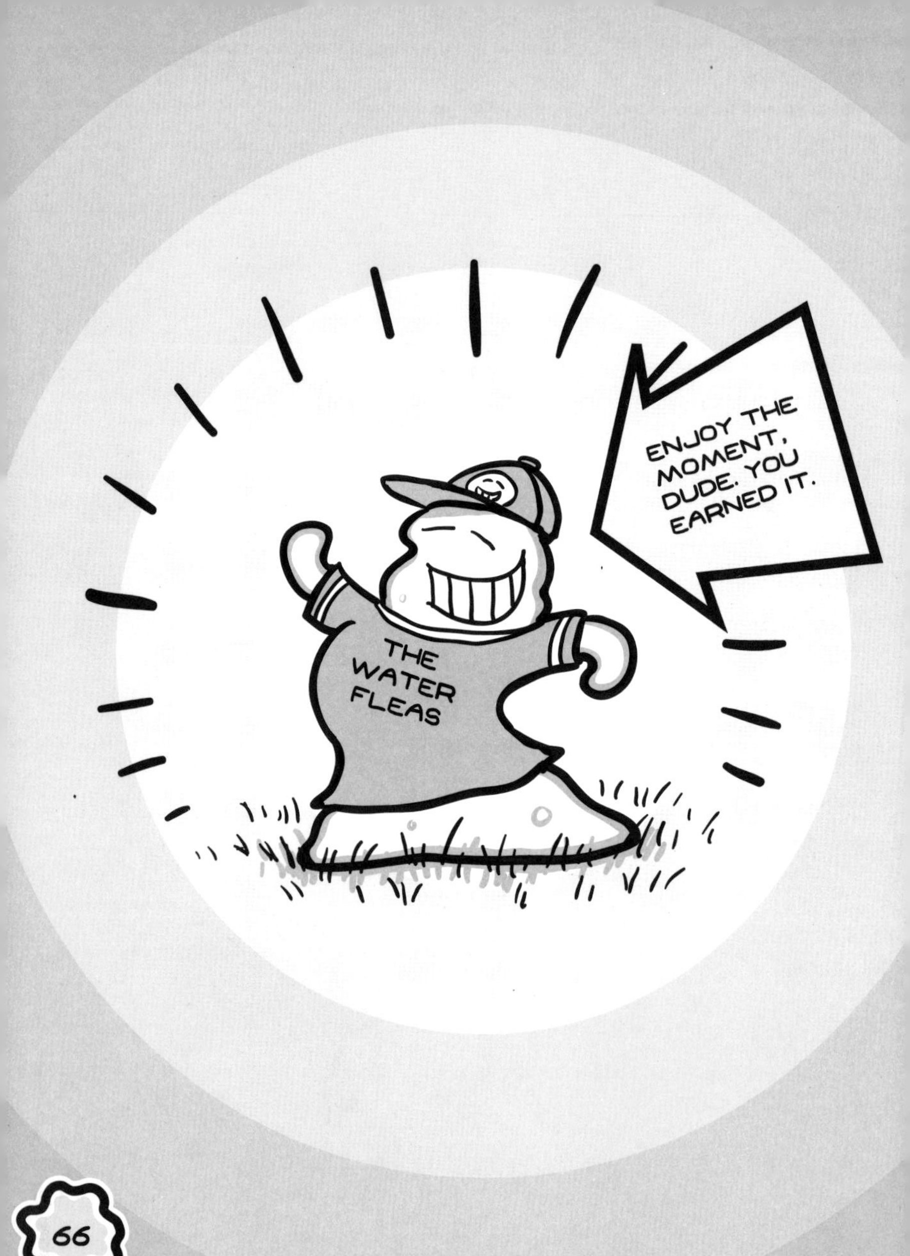
ENJOY THE MOMENT, DUDE. YOU EARNED IT.
THE WATER FLEAS

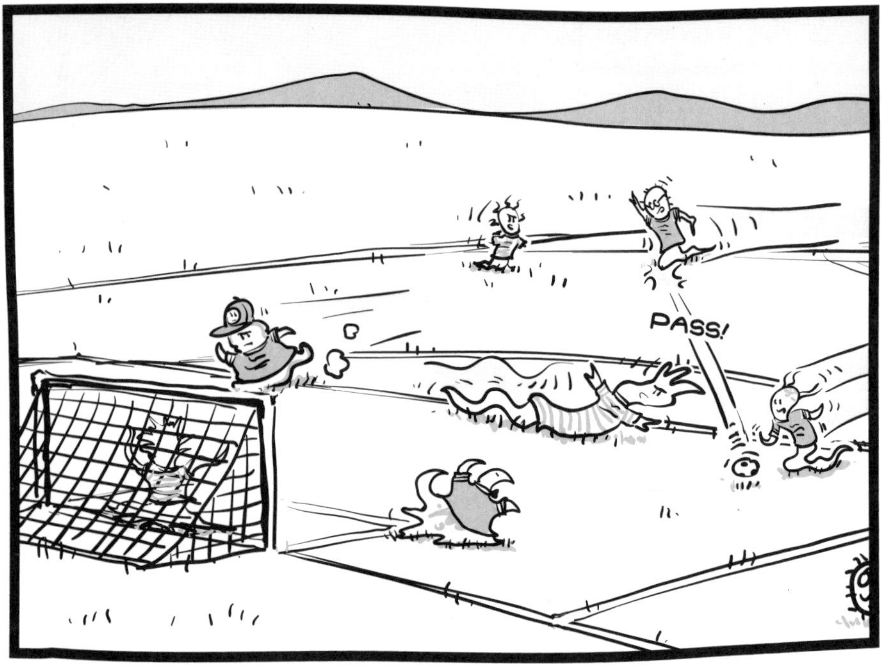
PASS!

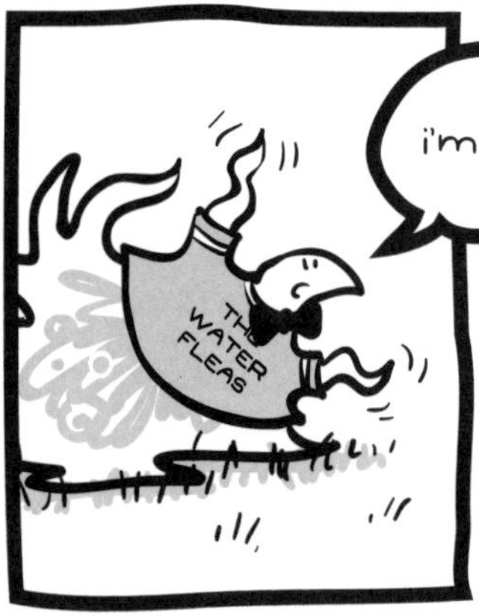
i'm open.
THE WATER FLEAS

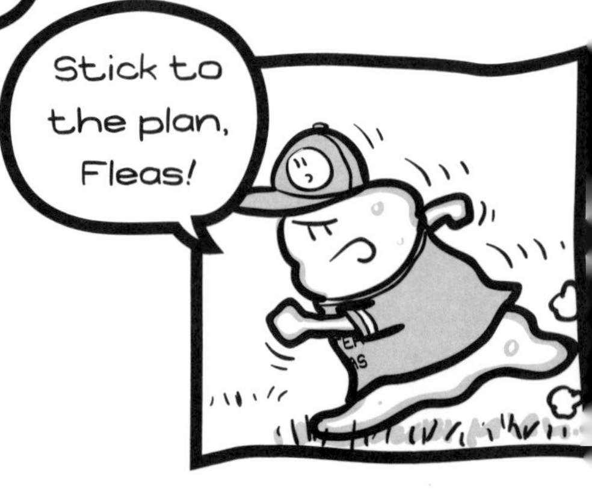
Stick to the plan, Fleas!

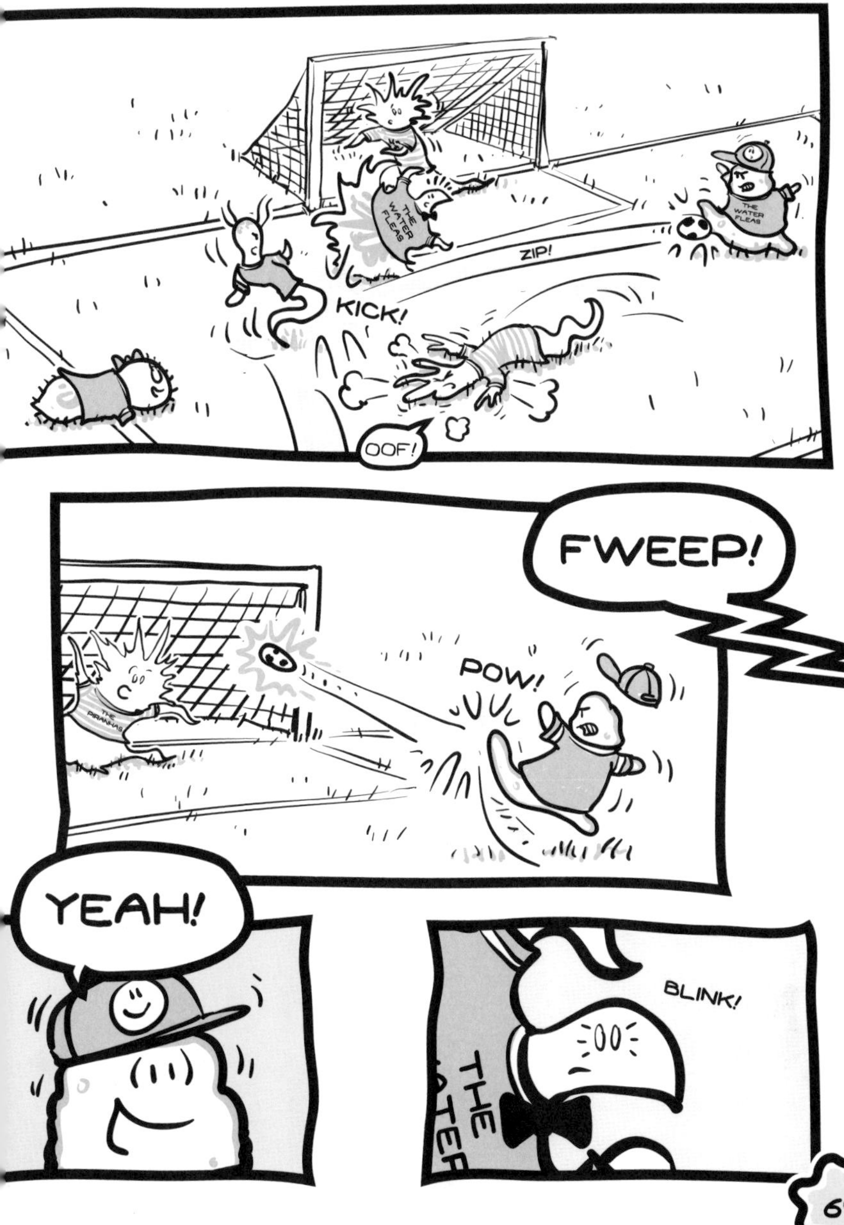
THE WATER FLEAS
THE WATER FLEAS
ZIP!
KICK!
OOF!
FWEEP!
THE PIRANHAS
POW!
YEAH!
BLINK!
THE WATER

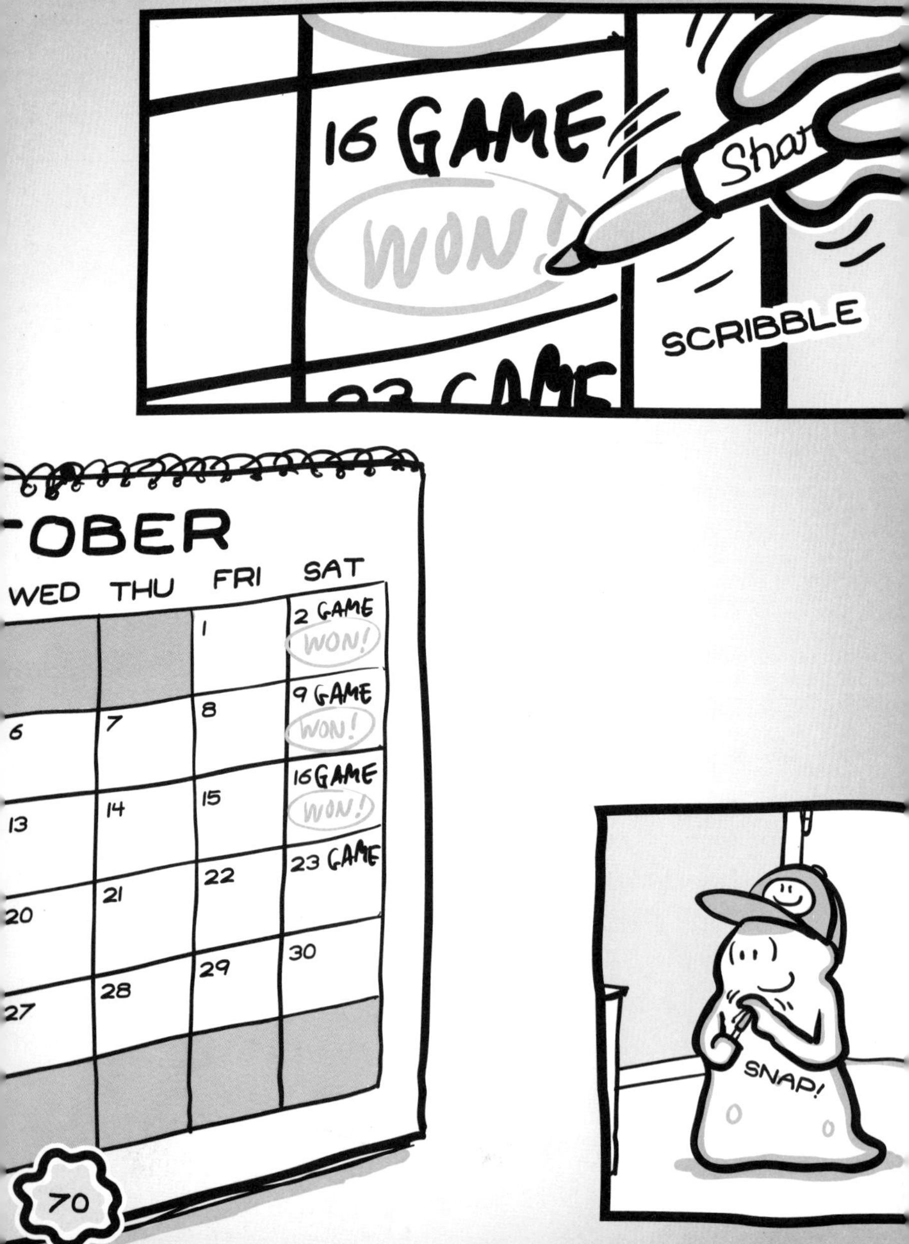
16 GAME
WON!
SCRIBBLE
WED THU FRI SAT
2 GAME
WON!
9 GAME
WON!
16 GAME
WON!
23 GAME
SNAP!

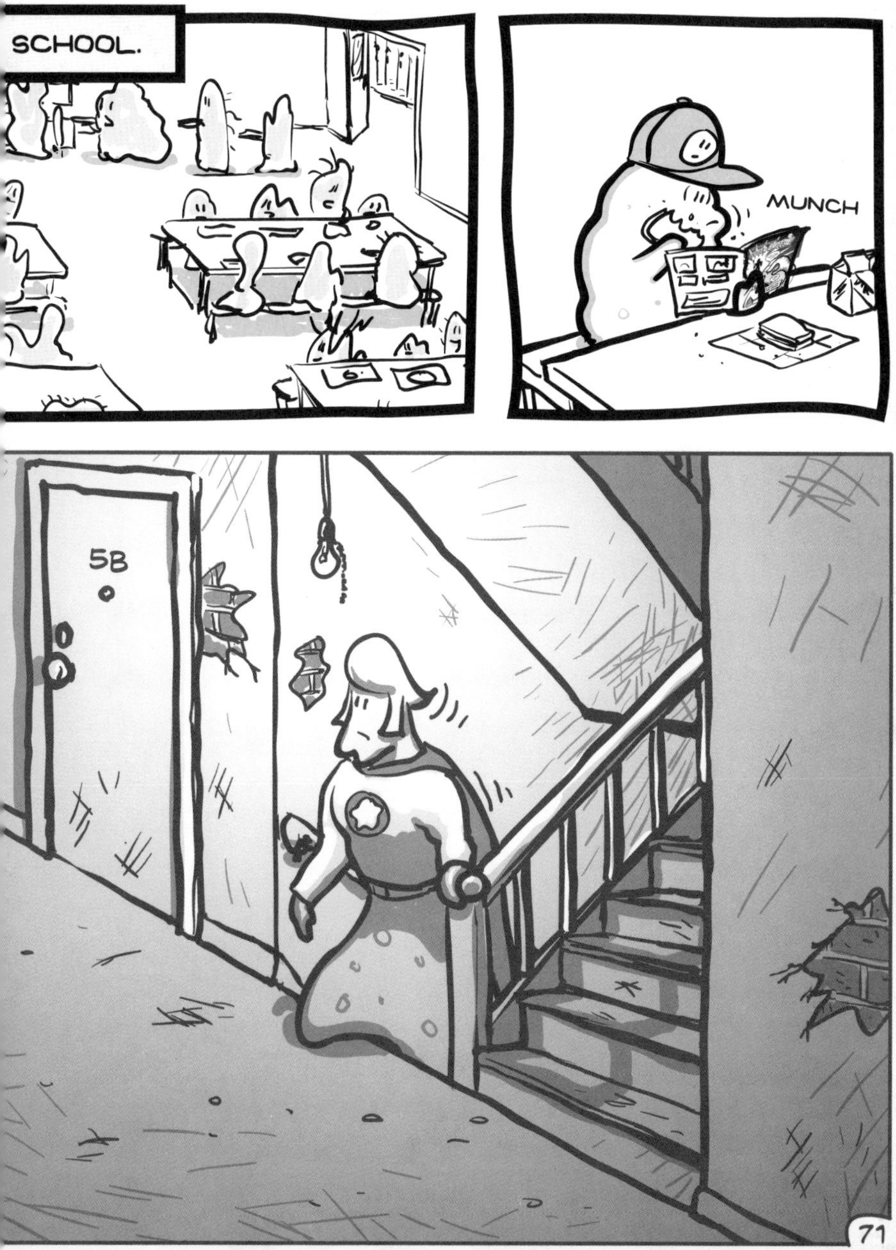
SCHOOL.
MUNCH
5B

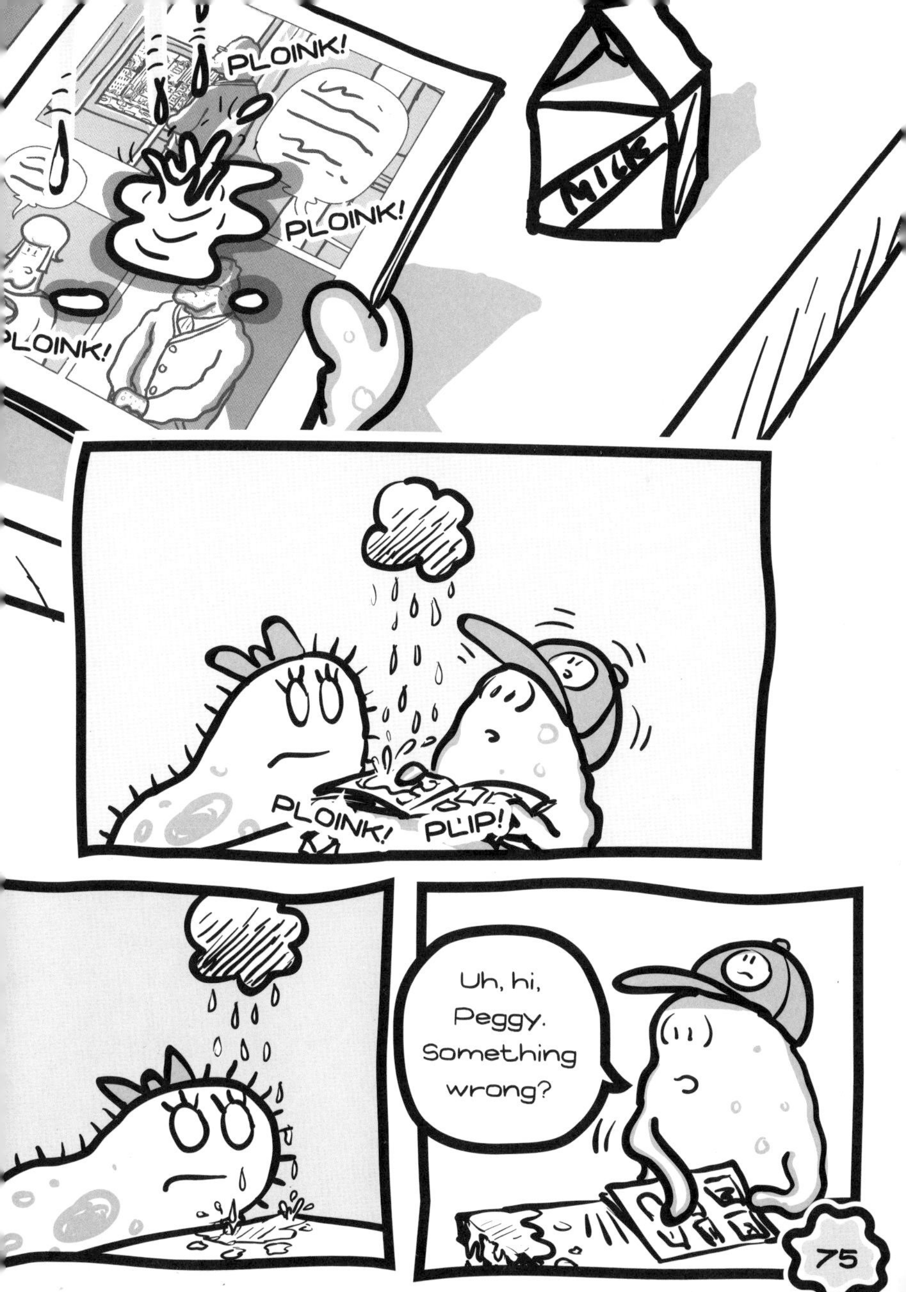

PLOINK!
PLOINK!
PLOINK!
MILK
PLOINK!
PLIP!
Uh, hi, Peggy. Something wrong?

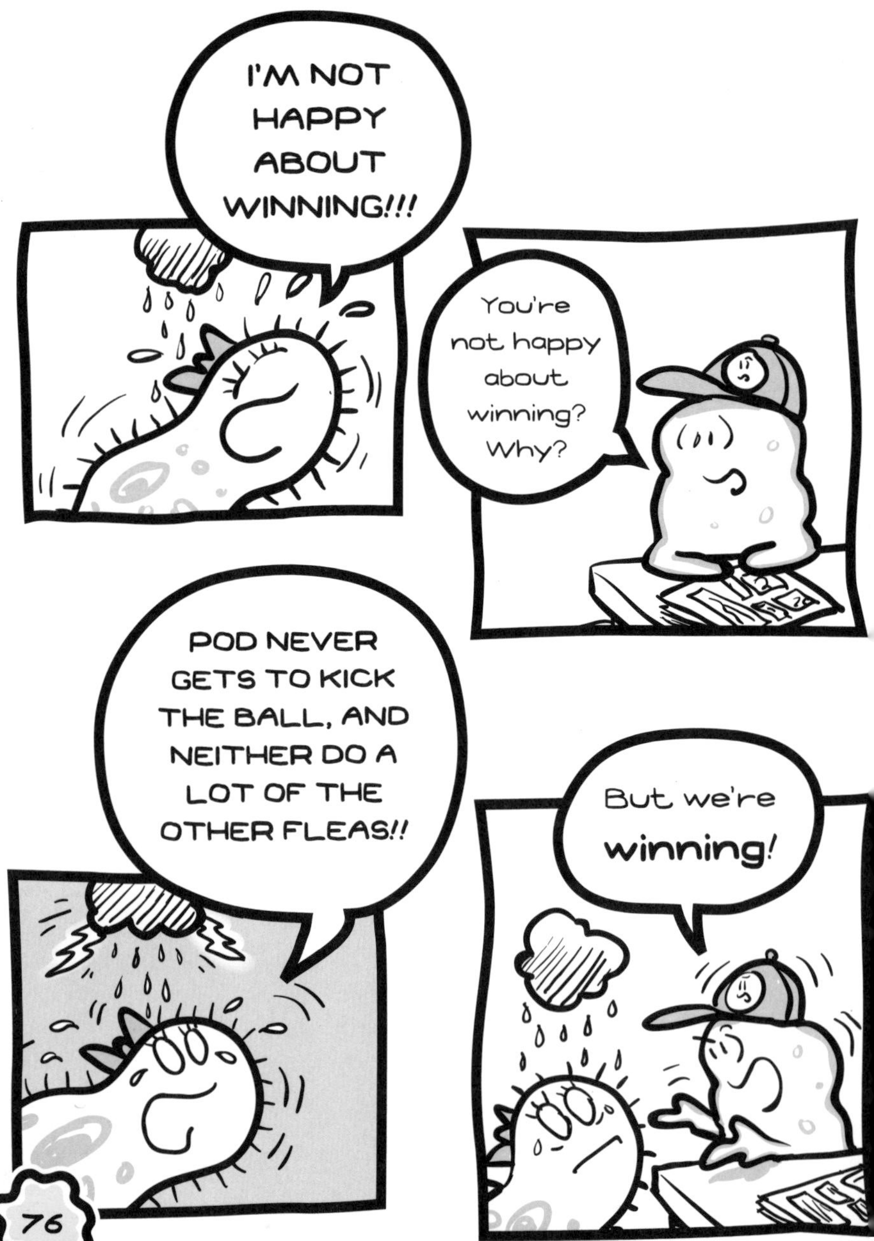
I'M NOT HAPPY ABOUT WINNING!!!
You're not happy about winning? Why?
POD NEVER GETS TO KICK THE BALL, AND NEITHER DO A LOT OF THE OTHER FLEAS!!
But we're **winning**!

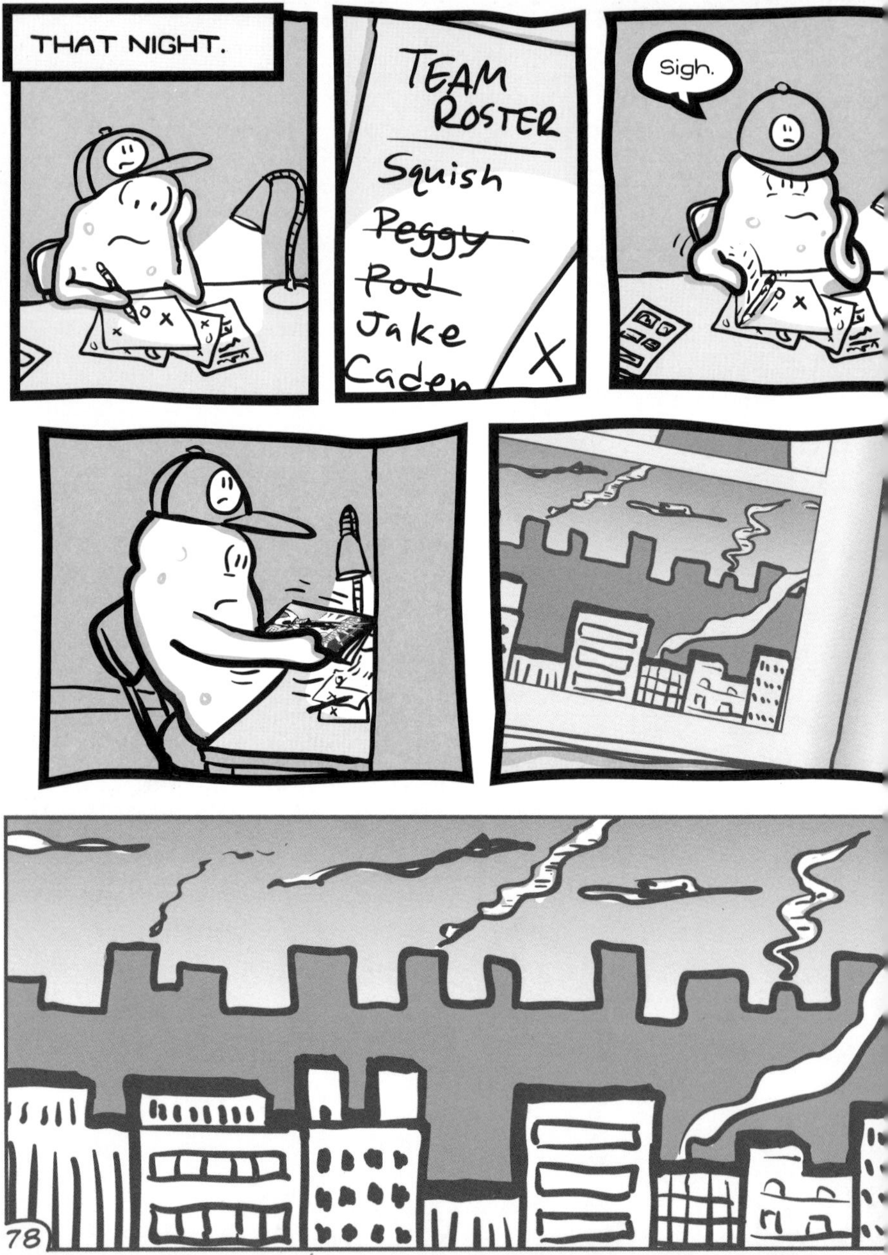
THAT NIGHT.
TEAM ROSTER
Squish
Peggy
Rod
Jake
Caden
Sigh.

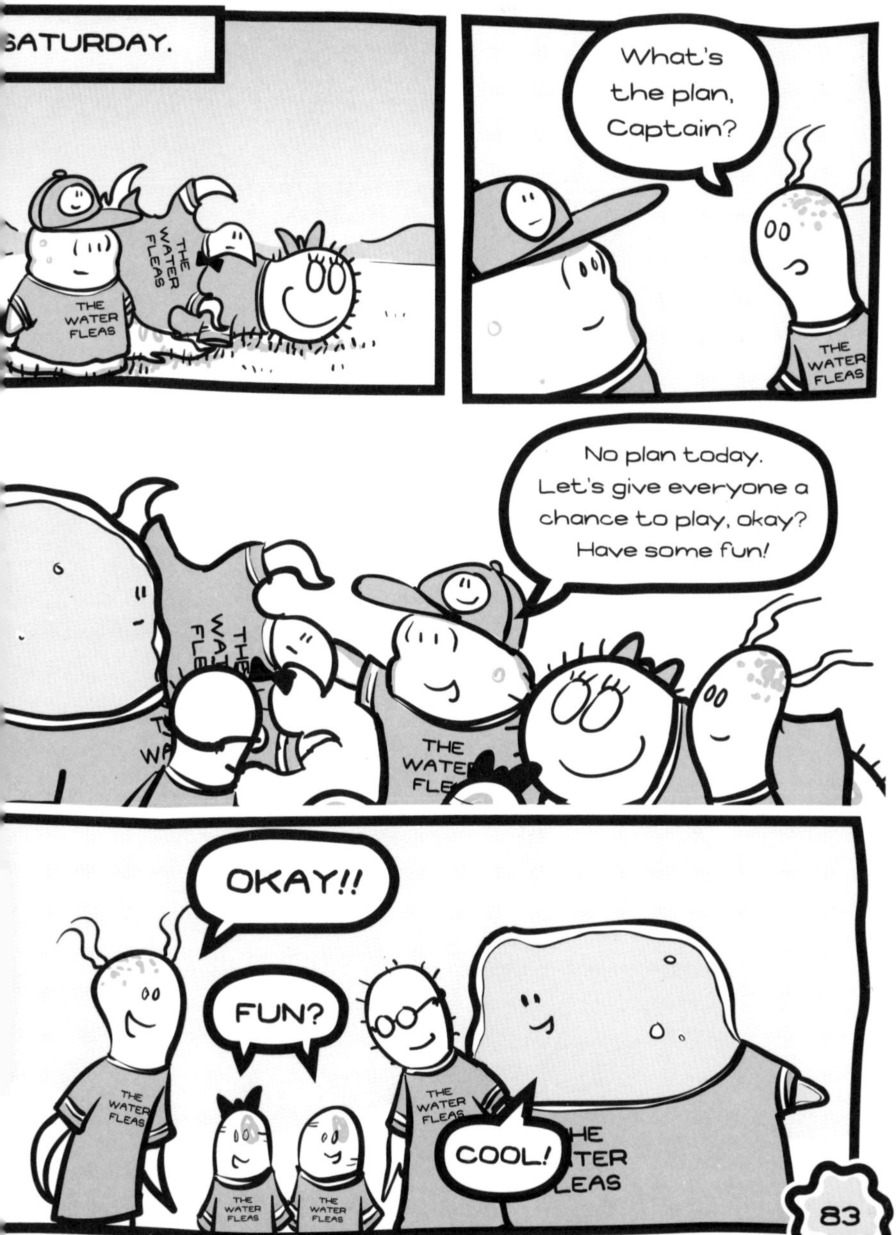
SATURDAY.
THE WATER FLEAS
What's the plan, Captain?
No plan today. Let's give everyone a chance to play, okay? Have some fun!
OKAY!!
FUN?
COOL!

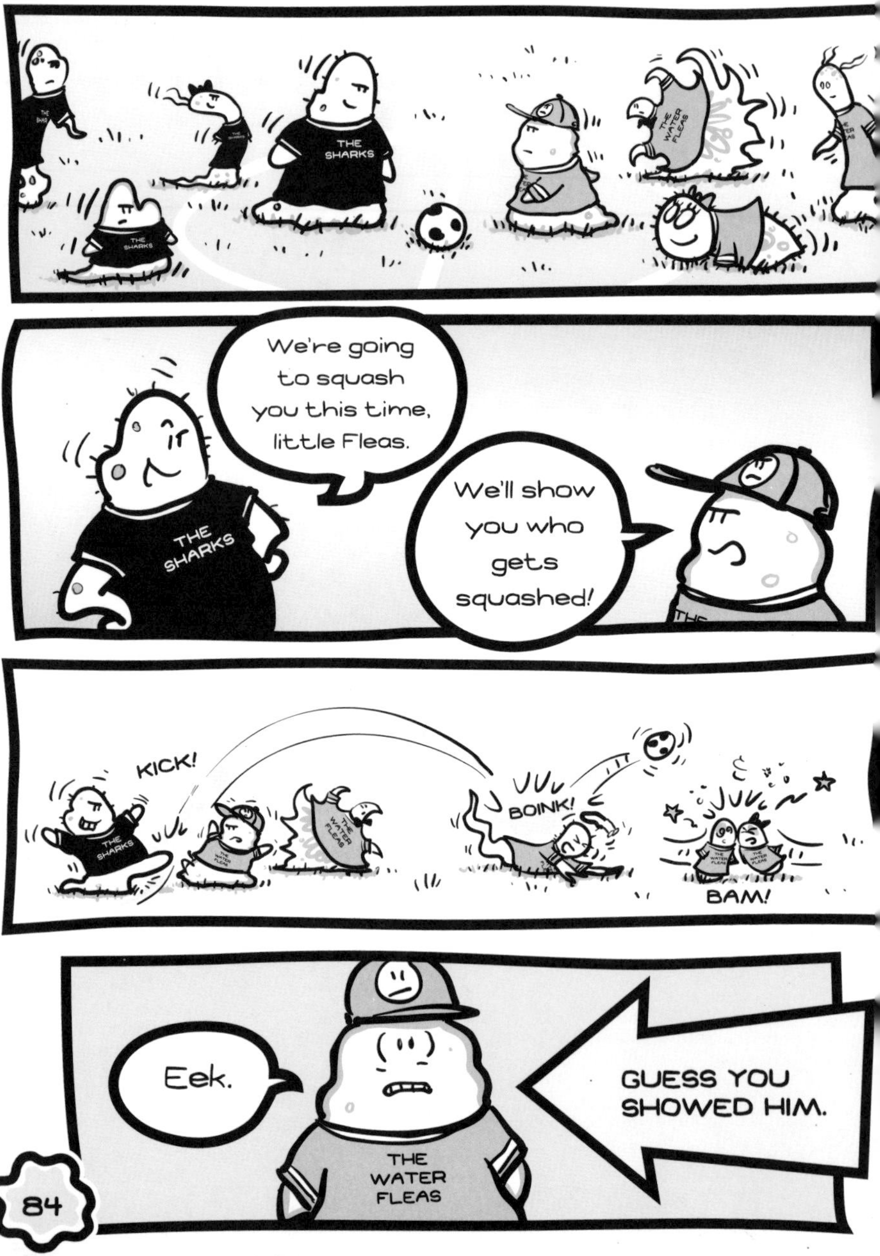
THE SHARKS
THE WATER FLEAS
We're going to squash you this time, little Fleas.
We'll show you who gets squashed!
KICK!
BOINK!
BAM!
Eek.
GUESS YOU SHOWED HIM.
THE WATER FLEAS

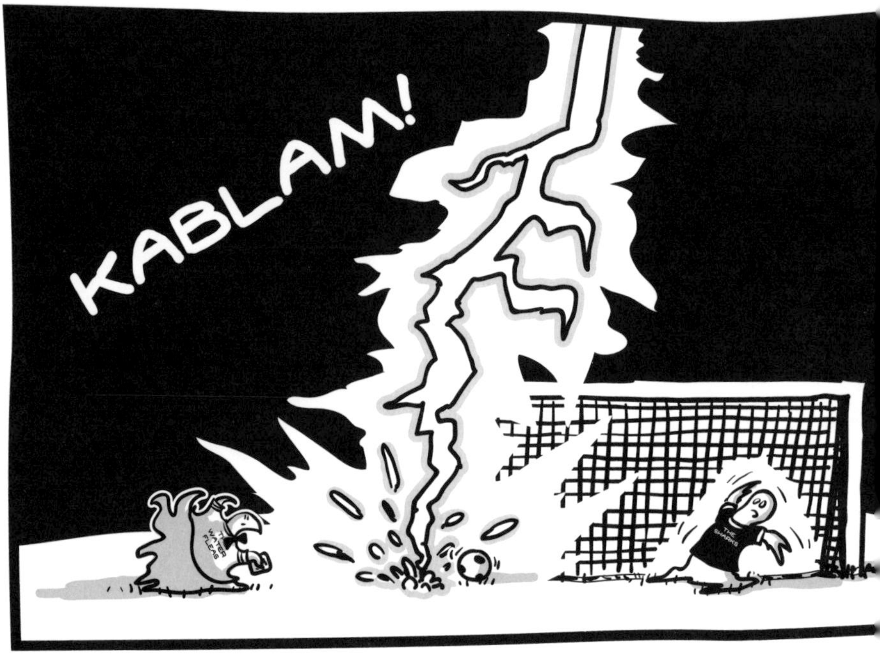
KABLAM!
WATER FLEAS
THE SHARKS

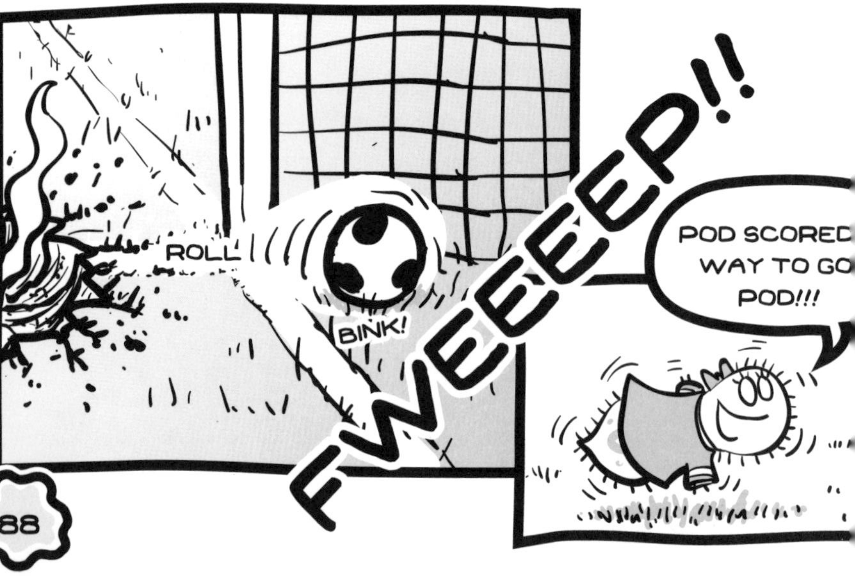
ROLL
BINK!
FWEEEEEP!!
POD SCORED WAY TO GO POD!!!

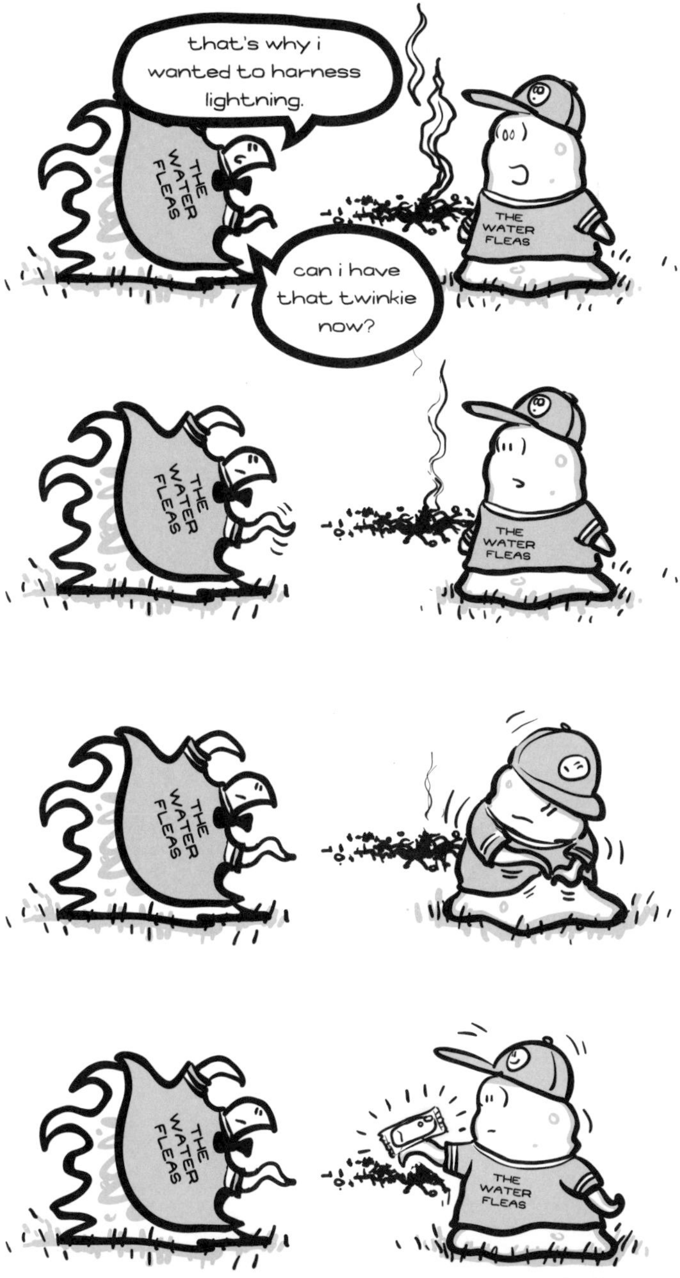

that's why i wanted to harness lightning.
THE WATER FLEAS
THE WATER FLEAS
can i have that twinkie now?
THE WATER FLEAS
THE WATER FLEAS
THE WATER FLEAS
THE WATER FLEAS
THE WATER FLEAS

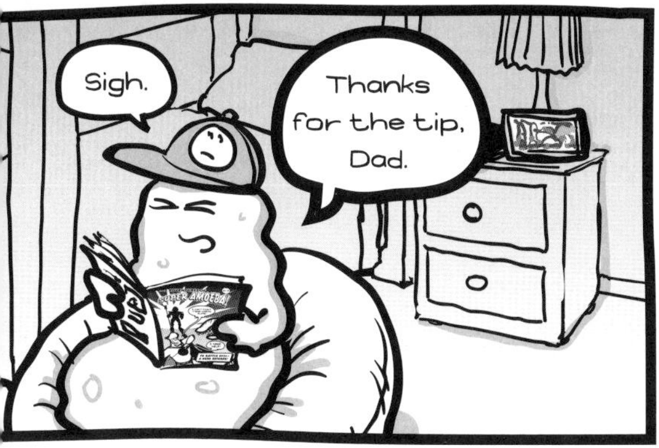
Sigh.
Thanks for the tip, Dad.

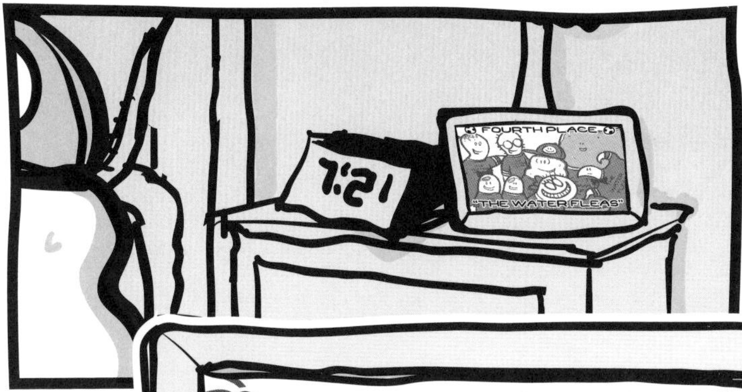
7:21
FOURTH PLACE
"THE WATER FLEAS"

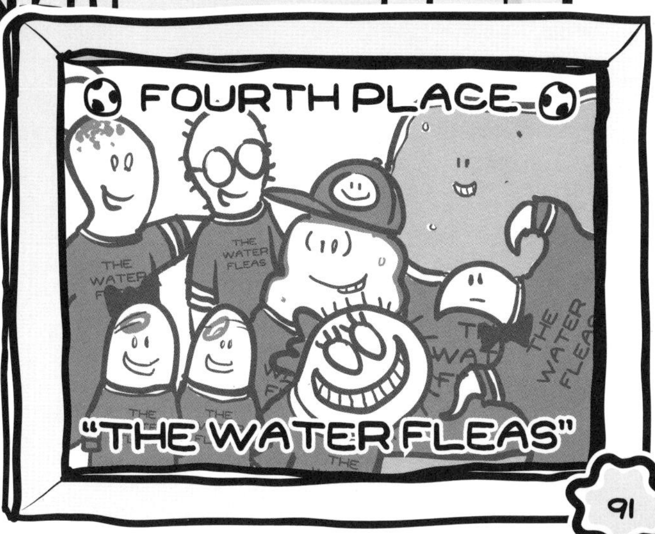
FOURTH PLACE
THE WATER FLEAS
THE WATER FLEAS
"THE WATER FLEAS"